PRAISE FOR THE *NEW YORK TIMES* BESTSELLING
FARMERS' MARKET MYSTERIES

Merry Market Murder

"One of my favorite series . . . Paige Shelton has put a real clever spin on the clues."   —*Escape with Dollycas into a Good Book*

"A perfect balance between murder and merriment . . . A great addition to a wonderful series."   —*Debbie's Book Bag*

A Killer Maize

"Masterfully plotted . . . A jam-packed whodunit that will 'a-maize' you!"   —*Escape with Dollycas into a Good Book*

"[A] darn good murder mystery."   —MyShelf.com

"The mystery is complex and captivating . . . The pace is quick. The plot is tight and fun. And Shelton's writing is a joy to read; her prose has an easy rhythm to it, her narrative style is both witty and engaging, and her dialogue is snappy and rings true."
                                                                —*The Season*

Crops and Robbers

"Shelton has dished up yet another tasty mystery . . . Readers will also get a nice taste of a potential love triangle between Becca's artsy love interest and the principled police officer who's willing to wait in the wings."   —*Mojave Desert News*

continued . . .

"Very fascinating . . . First-class writing and characterizations along with a lot of homegrown food and jam and jellies that will make your mouth water." —*Once Upon a Romance*

"I have loved this entire series . . . No matter the weather outside it is always a perfect time to visit Bailey's Farmers' Market and catch up with all the characters that have sprouted warmly in our hearts." —*Escape with Dollycas into a Good Book*

Fruit of All Evil

"A delicious mystery to be savored . . . [A] delightful continuation of the story line featuring feisty and smart amateur sleuth Becca Robins." —*Fresh Fiction*

"Spunky Becca should appeal to fans of Laura Childs and Joanne Fluke." —*Publishers Weekly*

"Fun characters and a great setting are the highlights of this series full of homegrown goodness." —*The Mystery Reader*

"A unique setting and interesting characters . . . You can enjoy Paige Shelton's Farmers' Market Mysteries for the stories, the characters, the humor. *Fruit of All Evil* beautifully blends all of those elements in a delightful mystery." —*Lesa's Book Critiques*

Farm Fresh Murder

"Watching jam-maker Becca Robins handle sticky situations is a tasty delight."
—Sheila Connolly, *New York Times* bestselling author of *An Early Wake*

"Becca is a genial heroine, and Shelton fashions a puzzling and satisfying whodunit. The first in a projected series, *Farm Fresh Murder* is a tasty treat." —*Richmond Times-Dispatch*

Bushel Full of Murder

PAIGE SHELTON

BERKLEY PRIME CRIME, NEW YORK

THE BERKLEY PUBLISHING GROUP
Published by the Penguin Group
Penguin Group (USA) LLC
375 Hudson Street, New York, New York 10014

USA • Canada • UK • Ireland • Australia • New Zealand • India • South Africa • China

penguin.com

A Penguin Random House Company

BUSHEL FULL OF MURDER

A Berkley Prime Crime Book / published by arrangement with the author

Berkley Prime Crime Books are published by The Berkley Publishing Group.
BERKLEY® PRIME CRIME and the PRIME CRIME logo are trademarks of
Penguin Group (USA) LLC.

For information, address: The Berkley Publishing Group,
a division of Penguin Group (USA) LLC,
375 Hudson Street, New York, New York 10014.

ISBN: 978-0-425-27980-9

PUBLISHING HISTORY
Berkley Prime Crime mass-market edition / June 2015

PRINTED IN THE UNITED STATES OF AMERICA

10 9 8 7 6 5 4 3 2 1

Cover illustration by Dan Craig.
Interior text design by Kristin del Rosario.

For my three main guys—Chuck, Charlie, and Tyler.
I love you.

Acknowledgments

A giant thank-you to—

My agent, Jessica Faust, who somehow continues to make me think she studied at Hogwarts and has mastered all sorts of magic.

My editor, Michelle Vega, who works untiringly to make each and every word count.

The cover artist for the Farmers' Market Mysteries, Dan Craig. He's perfect.

This is a place used to thank the people who helped you with the book that follows these first pages. I'm going to take some liberty with this one and use some space to send out a giant personal thank-you to Jessica, Michelle, and my precious family, friends, and readers. When my life was rocked with a personal crisis (about a year and a half ago from when this book publishes), you were all there to support and care. I can't express how much that still means to me, and I have no doubt that it was your support that gave my family the boost we needed to make it through. I will be forever grateful.

ON THE RUN

"Come on, Peyton, pull over," I said as I looked for something to hold on to. There were no handles anywhere, and the dashboard was just a flat piece of vinyl-covered plastic with a duct-taped heating and cooling vent at the top corner. This was one old truck. Even older than mine. But that wasn't fair; this truck did things mine didn't. It was an old box truck, but it had been converted to make food—delicious food, hot dogs topped with every imaginable thing, even things that shouldn't taste good on hot dogs.

"I'm innocent, Becca. You should know that. I can't get caught. They've made me look guilty. I have to get away and let things settle."

Her protests made her sound both irrationally panicked *and* guilty. But murder? Peyton? I looked at my cousin's profile. She was young, barely twenty-two, and pretty in a classic, perfect skin way. Though her short, dark curls were worn in a modern style, there was something reminiscent of the 1920s about her. Thin, sleek, with dainty features, a cute button nose, and a bow mouth. She was the baby of all the cousins. At first when she'd moved to Arizona to "find herself," we were all worried. But when we heard about the food truck, we hoped her journey of self-discovery had proved successful and she'd found a way to have a fulfilling career and life. This beautiful, smart free spirit couldn't be a killer, could she?

"Peyton, we're in a box truck. It's not built to go fast, and you shouldn't push it; it's too old, it's dangerous. It's a high-exposure vehicle, and a gust of wind or a quick turn could tip us over," I said as held on to the sides of the old seat. The truck was probably at its top speed, which was maybe about sixty-five, but it was so big and clunky that it bounced all around as we moved down the road. I hoped the brakes worked.

"It's the middle of June. There's no wind to tip us, Becca. And the sooner we get out of town, the better. I need to leave the jurisdiction. Your boyfriend and that other officer are bound and determined to make me look guilty."

"Peyton," I said, my voice sharp. I'd tried to be patient with my young cousin and her unusual behavior over the past few days, but she'd just hit my next to last nerve. I had only one left, and I really didn't want it triggered. "Sam is fair and will listen to everything you have to say. He doesn't jump to conclusions. Harry Lindon's also a friend and I'm sure he's fair, too."

"Sorry." She wasn't. "But come on, don't you think someone is trying to frame me?"

"I don't know, but Sam and Harry will make sure you are treated fairly," I repeated, my voice even sharper. "Pull. The. Truck. Over." I reached into my pocket and grabbed my cell phone.

We weren't far out of Monson, but once we were on the road, the passing scenery had turned into countryside quickly. We were on the way to Columbia, but there were many woods and farms and towns to pass by before we got there. I knew we were about to hit a big stretch ahead that didn't have any cell phone coverage, and I wanted to get ahold of Sam before we got there.

But I was too late. My phone had zero bars, which currently felt like less than zero. I glanced out the side window, but any thought to jump out of the truck withered quickly. Injury and pain were certain.

"Let's just get to the coast. I'll catch a cruise ship or something and leave the country," Peyton said.

I laughed. I couldn't help myself. "You've seen too many movies. That's not going to work. We're not even going to make it to Columbia. I'm going to call Sam and tell him what's going on."

"Becca, please! Just listen to me a minute. I'm not guilty. Someone is framing me. Okay, well, yes, I got into some trouble in Arizona, but I thought I got it cleared up. I can't explain that to Officer Lindon—he might be the one framing me, don't you see? And this . . . murder? Not in a million years, Becca. How could anyone think I had it in me to kill someone?"

"You won't be in trouble if you are innocent."

"But the evidence makes me look guilty. I will be arrested.

And if I'm arrested, I can't to do what needs to be done to clear my name. I need to get away. Why can't you understand that?"

"I understand, and I'll help, Peyton. Allison will help, so will my parents. You know them. They're all about making sure no one is wrongly accused of anything. They'll make signs and picket if they have to."

"No. Give me that phone." Peyton reached over quickly and tried to grab the phone out of my hands.

I pulled back, but the moving and rocking truck didn't make it easy. The phone fell onto the flat, dirty metal floor beneath my feet.

"Stop it, Peyton," I said as I bent over and tried to grab the phone.

I hadn't put on the flimsy seat belt. Supporting myself with my feet as I bent over to reach for the phone was precarious. The floor was slippery enough that the phone zipped back and forth, continually dodging my reach. Peyton jerked the steering wheel so it would slide close to her toes.

"Peyton! Come on!"

Another steering wheel jerk and the phone disappeared under the driver's seat, out of my fingers' and Peyton's toes' reach.

"Stop the truck, Peyton, and let's just talk about this a minute. Give me a chance to understand your position better. No one is after us right now. No one knows where we are. Just explain to me what's going on. I'm on your side. You know I am."

I tried to sound sincere, but I wasn't sure I pulled it off. Mostly I wanted to punch her.

Peyton looked over at me. Her brown eyes were panicked and scared, and suddenly I did feel a small but genuine drop of sympathy for her. She was young. She was terrified. It was a combination that frequently led to bad decisions.

"Please," I said.

She nodded and looked back at the road.

But even though she'd had her eyes off the road for only a second, it was enough to cause the truck to travel over the yellow line. And even though there wasn't much traffic on these back roads, there were some cars in the opposite lane. We suddenly faced a big, red, horn-honking pickup truck. I tried to brace myself on something and Peyton screamed as she jerked the steering wheel.

One more time.

One

FOUR DAYS EARLIER

"Close your eyes," he said.

I did as he instructed.

"Okay, stick out your tongue," he said.

I did.

"Tell me what you think." He deposited a small drop of liquid onto my tongue.

"Mmm," I said a second later. "That is so good. Can I open my eyes?"

"Sure."

Herb and Don, of Herb and Don's Herbs, a popular stall at Bailey's Farmers' Market, stood in front of my stall with expectant looks on their faces and a collection of dark brown miniature bottles in their hands.

"Really good," I said. "That's your peppermint?"

"It is, and made into our very own peppermint oil. So good. Right?" Don asked. "Flavorful, maybe even a little cooling?" He smiled. Even if the peppermint had been served with a sliver of ice, it would have done very little to combat today's heat and humidity.

"Yes," I said, returning the smile. "It's perfect." I knew exactly what it was like to bring a new product to the market. Nerve-wracking. I'd done a few taste test tours through Bailey's aisles myself. There were never enough positive comments, never enough assurances that the product you'd created was a good one, and one that would not only sell, but that customers would sincerely enjoy.

"Oh, good," Herb said, his shoulders relaxing. He grinned at Don. "She likes it."

"She does," Don said with his own smile. "We're at one hundred percent, Becca. Everyone who has tried it has given us good reviews, but we were most worried about you. You have one of the best tasters at the market."

"I did not know that. Glad I could help."

"When Ian said he could show us how to create essential oils from some of our herbs, we thought we were in for a terrible learning curve, but he's helped us so much." Don's smile faded. He blinked and bit his bottom lip. It took me a second, but I figured out the problem: he wasn't sure he should side with Ian in front of me on anything ever again. I appreciated his loyalty.

I laughed. "Ian and I are still friends. Ian and Sam are

friends, too. It's good"—I leaned toward them—"but between me and you guys, it's also a little weird."

It really wasn't all that weird, my old boyfriend and my new boyfriend having a friendly relationship of their own, but I knew it should be weird so that's usually what I told people. In fact, Ian, my old (much younger) boyfriend, and Sam, my current and forever boyfriend (or so I hoped), seemed to get along great. They genuinely liked each other. There was a point, early on in my relationship with Sam, that I was sure he would put a halt to our dating if Ian had been adamant about wanting to stay with me. I thought that maybe we'd passed that point, and that Sam would now fight until the bitter end for me, or at least put Ian in a jail cell until the younger man came to his senses.

Sam was a Monson police officer so he had access to a couple small holding cells in the back room at the police station. Ian was in his mid-twenties and an artist with long hair and lots of tattoos, but none of the criminal behavior that might be expected to stereotypically coincide with that look. Instead, he was a smart, ambitious, talented yard art artist and lavender farmer, with plans to make all sorts of products from his crops—essential oils were only the beginning. Not long ago he'd mentioned to me that Herb and Don were becoming interested in his oil development techniques, and he was excited to teach them his ways. I was happy to see that the end result of their project together had become a viable new market product.

"I'm so glad to hear that. You know, things don't seem weird around here with you and Ian, but he's at the market less and less and we just weren't sure. We should have just asked, huh?" Don said.

"It's okay. I understand."

Herb and Don were both business and life partners and had had an herb stall at Bailey's for years. They'd been so successful growing oregano that they'd been approached by a national spice company, and both of them were offered great-paying jobs in the product development department. But they declined, choosing to stay at Bailey's instead of going to what they predicted was a sterile indoor environment requiring adherence to corporate rules and such. We'd all been happy to hear the good news.

"Thank you, Becca," Herb said. "When we have the oil ready for sale, we'll drop off a bottle for you."

"I'd love one."

Ah, the perks of working at a farmers' market.

Herb and Don dodged customers as they continued down the aisle in search of other available vendor tongues. I glanced over my inventory. Six jars of strawberry preserves were all that was left for the day, and my regular customers and special orders had all been taken care of and reordered if necessary. I was tempted to pack up the jars and go home, or to someplace where I could jump into frigid water, maybe step into a freezer.

My fraternal twin sister and the Bailey's manager, Allison, had installed a tubed water mister system along the aisles and above the stalls that had given us tiny clouds of cooling relief during our warm South Carolina summer temperatures, but the misters had stopped working the day before. She'd been trying to get someone to come out and fix them since only a few seconds after they'd come to a silent and dry halt, giving way to a collective moan of despair that spread throughout the market.

We'd been spoiled by our misters.

Unfortunately, Allison couldn't be her typical determined pest with the repair people because another surprise had been sprung on her only a few hours ago.

Bailey's managers had given the go-ahead for five food trucks to spend two weeks in the market's parking lot, and the trucks were scheduled to arrive today. They were part of a national program called KEEP ON EATING. The participants were reimbursed all fuel and hotel expenses as they traveled to someplace that they'd never served their food before, preferably away from their home states. It was a way to bring attention to the food truck industry, different regional foods, as well as to some of the unknown but talented chefs and bakers who created delicious, in some cases gourmet, food—from inside a truck. The benefits to Bailey's were hopefully increased traffic to the market, and an agreement that the food truck operators would purchase as many groceries as they could from the market vendors. The chefs would place signs on their trucks mentioning that they were only using the best-quality and freshest food, found locally from Bailey's Farmers' Market. It was with the delivery of the signs earlier today that Allison learned about the trucks' imminent arrival.

It was a great idea, of course, no matter how or when the news had been delivered. But unfortunately, making sure the goings-on went off without a hitch was more than just making sure there was room in the parking lot for the trucks. Allison's duties had been all about KEEP ON EATING since the moment she'd seen the signs. I hadn't talked to her since, but I had left her a phone message letting her know that if she needed any help, I could make myself available.

So instead of going home, I decided I would pack up my remaining inventory and then track down my sister. Maybe she actually could use a hand but hadn't had a moment to call me back.

I grabbed a box from underneath my front table and started to load the six jars.

"Ms. Robins?" A voice that seemed hesitant but familiar pulled my attention back up toward the aisle.

I recognized him. I remembered him. But how was he here? How was he in South Carolina? It didn't fit. His deeply tanned skin and brown eyes—framed in the best laugh lines I'd ever seen—his thick, dark hair, the ever-present cowboy hat. Had he taken a wrong turn or gotten lost, perhaps somewhere around Missouri?

"Hi! Oh my gosh!" I said as I abandoned the box and the jars and stepped around my front table to greet my friend from Arizona. "Harry! Talking Trees! It's great to see you."

"Becca Robins, hello," Harry said with a smile that crinkled the laughing lines into deep cheery fan folds.

Harry Lindon, also known as Talking Trees on his reservation home in Arizona, was a law enforcement officer in his neck of the woods; his hot, dry, desert neck of the woods. I'd visited Chief Buffalo's Trading Post and Farmers' Market the summer before and had met Harry when murder had become a part of the adventure.

"You look well. Good as new," I said. "What in the world are you doing in South Carolina?"

"I'm fine," he said, waving away any concern I might have about his state of health or his recovery from the potentially deadly injuries I knew he'd suffered. "I'm here on business, but I was surprised and happy when I heard I was coming to Monson so I could see my new friend who made me laugh even after we'd gone through some very dangerous moments together."

"I'm so happy to see you, too. What in the world would your business be in South Carolina?"

Harry looked around. He was tall, but not as tall as his presence made him seem. His wide shoulders and cowboy hat made it feel like he took up a gigantic amount of space.

"This is not a great place to talk. Maybe I could buy you a cup of coffee, or something cold to drink after you're done working?" he said.

"I'm done," I said. I felt bad about not tracking down Allison, but I couldn't resist taking some time to understand why Harry was in Monson, here on "business." "Do you have a vehicle?"

"I flew into Columbia and then rented a car. It's out front in the lot."

"I have an orange truck. I'll come around and then you can follow me to a coffee shop."

"All right," Harry said.

Only a few minutes later, I'd officially closed my stall for the day and brought my truck around to the front parking lot. Harry waited at the entrance in his tiny car. His hat was off because there couldn't possibly be enough room for both him and it.

I led us to Maytabee's, a local coffee shop, one of six now in South Carolina that carried some of my products. My preserves, jams, and jellies had sold well from the first day they'd been on the Maytabee's shelves, but lately they'd done even better, orders coming in twice as big as they'd been only a few months earlier. I didn't mind, even with the now required extra hours spent in my converted barn/kitchen.

I was dressed in my typical summer short overalls and it had been a hot day, so the overalls and my short blond hair were both wilted, but the people at Maytabee's had seen me in even worse shape—in fact, one day extra-blue from a jar of blueberry jam I'd dropped in the parking lot when it had slipped out of my hurried hands. They'd referred to me as the Oompa Loompa jam lady ever since.

I didn't recognize any of the baristas today, though, as I asked Harry to take a seat while I ordered the coffees.

We sat across from each other in matching worn leather chairs, both of us able to enjoy the cool air coming from a ceiling vent. The chairs were off in a corner by themselves, so though there were a few other customers in the shop none were close enough to hear our conversation.

Briefly, we recounted the craziness we'd gone through together in Arizona, but Harry didn't want to give me many details regarding the deeper investigation into the motives behind the murder of a Native American jewelry maker, other than to tell me that the authorities had the important answers but were still trying to get more details. I made him promise to call me and let me know once all the mysteries had been solved. He said he would.

"Harry, what is your business in Monson?" I finally asked.

"Ah, it's a curious thing, I suppose. I'm on the trail of

someone we think stole a substantial sum of money from a large restaurant in Arizona. She worked for them at the time, stole the money along with one of their proprietary recipes."

"And she's in Monson?"

"She's on her way, I think. I don't think she's arrived yet. I hope she truly does make it here. She operates a food truck—a venture she began shortly after leaving the restaurant. She got out of town too quickly for me. I was going to follow her, but I missed her middle-of-the-night exit a few nights ago."

"Food truck! I know about the food trucks. Five are coming in. But from Arizona? I can't imagine why someone would travel so far."

"It's a long way to go, but we think she's trying to get far away from home. We don't know if she's trying to make a permanent move or just a temporary one. When I contacted the organization sponsoring the summer food truck event, they told me that she requested Monson specifically. They said they tried to honor all of the requests they got, though most of the trucks were only going to travel a state or two away from their homes."

I knew nothing about the specific trucks set to arrive at Bailey's. I didn't know what kind of food they prepared, and other than selling them some of my products at a discount, I didn't know what role I was to play in their visit.

"Tell me more about her. What kind of food?"

"Gourmet hot dogs. They're good, too. She grills all the dogs. Her toppings are delicious, including the secret recipe she stole, a sauce made with tomatoes and a mix of spices that has just the right bite, but lots of flavor."

"Mmm. My mouth is watering."

"I have to admit when I started investigating the alleged stolen recipe, the part where I had to sample the food was much more enjoyable than lots of other investigations I've conducted."

"The sauce is identical?" I said.

"Mostly," he said hesitantly.

"Mostly?"

I was not in a position to interject any ideas into Harry's investigation. I didn't know the details, I didn't know the people involved. But I'd witnessed a few alleged recipe thefts over the years. When you work with food, even if it's not in a restaurant setting, you have the chance to taste things that are so good that you want to create something similar. It becomes a challenge, a goal. Recipe theft is one thing, but trying to re-create something based upon your own tastes and experience is something else altogether.

"Is that what makes you think she stole the recipe?" I asked.

"It started when the card with the secret recipe went missing from the restaurant's office. She was the last one seen leaving the office. On her own, behaving suspiciously. The sequence of events is too long to go into now but that combined with her quick departure from the restaurant shortly thereafter and what happened to the manager the week before makes her look pretty guilty. I've been hanging around her truck trying to figure her out, as well as eating the food she prepares. It's very good. I started questioning her more seriously a couple weeks ago. I think she got nervous about my curiosity, and the food truck tour became a convenient way to leave town, at least for a little while."

"What happened to the restaurant manager?"

"She was assaulted on her way to the bank to make a deposit."

"Is she okay?"

"Concussion. Not good, but could be worse. She'll be okay eventually."

"That's good. Mind if I ask how much the deposit was? I'm just trying to get a feel for the size of the restaurant."

Harry looked at me with his intelligent brown eyes. They were such friendly eyes. Even when he'd been in the middle of some of the most terrifying moments life could throw your way, his eyes had remained friendly. I knew. I'd experienced some of the terror with him. Right now his friendly eyes told me that he was about to say something important. I listened closely.

"Fifty thousand dollars," Harry said quietly, no matter that no one was close enough to eavesdrop.

"Good grief!"

"The alleged thief had been put in charge of the restaurant the previous week. She claims that before the manager went on vacation, she told her not to take any deposits to the bank. The manager would take care of the money when she got back."

"That doesn't make sense."

"No, it doesn't, and the manager claims she never made that request."

"This is not looking good for the food truck woman."

"No, particularly when after the assault and the suspicious exit from the restaurant office, she was able to open her food truck. And with cash, from what I understand. There were no bank records of the money's movement until the seller of the food truck put it in her bank account."

"Why haven't you already arrested her?"

"It's still all circumstantial, Becca. No proof, but I'm working on it. Or I hope to somehow catch her either in her lies or doing something else illegal."

"Good luck. I hope you get her. What's her name? I'll keep an eye on her, too."

"Peyton Chase."

I'd never experienced a real choke-on-your-drink moment. When Harry said the chef's name, I hadn't even been taking a sip. Technically I guess I choked on the sharp intake of air that accompanied my gasp. The name was too unusual for it not to be attached to the person I thought it was attached to. Peyton. Arizona. Food truck. Until he'd said her name, I hadn't considered that my cousin might be a part of Harry's "business."

"Wait, did you say Peyton Chase?" I said after I recovered.

"I did. You okay?" He sat forward on the chair and set his coffee on the floor.

"Fine. Hang on one second, Harry," I said. I pulled out my phone and pushed the button for Allison. With whatever good juju I might have, I willed that she answer this time.

"Hey, Becs, what's up?" she said.

"Peyton Chase," I said.

"Yeah?"

"She's one of the food truck people."

"She is? Hang on." Allison must have been in her office. I heard papers shuffle and a drawer open and close. "Yes! The hot dog truck. I had no idea."

"Our Peyton Chase?" I said.

"I thought she was in Arizona, but if it's Peyton, who knows what she's up to? But why would she travel this far?"

"I think it's our Peyton, Allison."

"Okay. That's great!"

"Maybe."

"What do you mean?"

"I'll tell you later. Gotta go."

"Uh, okay. Well, the trucks should start arriving in about half an hour. Be here if you want."

"Will do." I ended the call and looked at Harry.

"What's going on, Becca?" he said. He hadn't removed his hat yet. He did now, setting it on the floor next to his coffee, punctuating the sudden seriousness of the moment.

"Harry, I have a cousin named Peyton Chase. I know she moved to Arizona in search of herself and an adventure. We were all pretty excited when we heard she got a food truck, but I never learned the details. I don't know if hers is a gourmet hot dog truck. I wonder if we're talking about the same Peyton. But . . . how could it not be?"

Harry reached into a small pocket with embroidered edging on the front of his vest and pulled out a picture.

"This her?" he said as he held it out for me to inspect.

The picture was a close-up of a young woman leaning out over the counter of the truck, serving someone a hot dog piled high with onions towering above the red and white paper boat the dog sat in. The woman's short, wavy, dark hair was held back by a blue bandanna and her eyes were just as happy as her big smile.

"Yes, that's her." My heart sank. I literally felt it plummet.

"I see." Harry sighed heavily and sat back on the chair.

He returned the picture to his pocket and then steepled his fingers, resting his chin on top. "I suppose there are some conflicts of interest arising here."

"Because you and I know each other?"

"Yes."

"So you won't be able to investigate thoroughly because you're friends with your suspect's cousin? We might be fast friends, Harry, but we only hung out a few days total."

"Someone might question the integrity of my investigation."

"I don't believe that. Again, I might not know you well or for long, but you don't let personal feelings get in the way of your investigations. I know that firsthand. I saw that. In Arizona, it got pretty personal for you, Harry."

"Still." Harry's eyebrows came together and he moved his hands to the chair's armrests.

"Hang on."

I needed to think about what I wanted to say. I knew what I was about to suggest wasn't the most usual way to handle the predicament in front of us. I'd been shaken by my cousin's potential involvement in illegal activities, but I still had enough of my wits about me to know that I didn't want Harry to relinquish his investigating duties to someone else. Harry waited patiently as I held up one finger and let my brain work through some needed gyrations.

"Harry, let me help you," I finally said after the pieces came together in my mind.

Harry laughed, transforming his serious face into a happy, amused one. "Becca, either you like or don't like your cousin. She's family, it can go either way. But whatever the case, you helping me doesn't make sense, and would only compromise the investigation even more."

"No, hear me out. My boyfriend, Sam, is a local police officer. I'll introduce you to him. He's like you—wouldn't let personal feelings get in the way of investigating a case, ever. You two can work on it together. I can help by trying to prove Peyton innocent, but Sam won't let me get in the way. You look for evidence of guilt; I'll look for evidence of innocence. I know that's not how it's supposed to work, but I do like Peyton, Harry. I love her. I haven't seen her for about five years, but I care deeply for my cousin. She was a sweet, kind, but somewhat untamed child who Allison and I probably tormented way too much, but she always had a determined attitude. I really hoped she'd find herself. She sure seemed to need to search a lot."

Harry couldn't hide his skepticism. His friendly chocolate eyes, it seemed, could squint perfectly with doubt. "I'm not sure that's the best way to go about this, but Arizona is a long way away, and it might be a challenge to get someone else from there interested enough to make the trip all the way here. All right, Becca, I'll give it a day or two."

"Great! This will work. Somehow, this will work." I lifted my coffee cup in a toast.

I just hoped it worked in Peyton's favor.

Two

The plan was to take Harry to the police station immediately and introduce him to Sam, but when I called to see if Sam was at the station, he told me he was actually at Bailey's, there to provide crowd assistance and suggestions regarding the placement of the soon-to-arrive food trucks. He'd quickly educated himself on town ordinances regarding the legal placement of all types of temporary businesses. I mentioned that I was surprised we had any such ordinances. He added that they were pretty vague.

Harry followed me back to Bailey's and we both parked in the front lot, on the side opposite of where it seemed the trucks would be parked. We concluded that something important must be going on over there considering the number of people who had gathered. Harry and I observed as we leaned, side by side, against Harry's petite rental car. The goal was to not draw attention to ourselves as we took a few minutes to get the "lay of the land." However, between Harry's hat and my orange truck, we were probably hard to miss.

"When you were in Arizona, you mentioned that your love life was . . . I think you used the word *messy*. At the coffee shop you said your boyfriend was a police officer. Sounds like you got things figured out."

"I did. Sam"—I nodded toward the other side of the parking lot where Sam stood with his hands on his hips next to Allison, inspecting a patch of open land next to the parking lot that extended to the back of this side of the market stalls and up to the two-lane highway—"and I have been together since shortly after I returned home from Arizona. It's not so messy or complicated anymore. In fact, it's as close to noncomplicated as I've ever been. The woman standing next to Sam is my sister, Allison."

"You two look nothing alike," Harry said.

I laughed. "Would you believe we're twins? Fraternal, of course. Allison is tall, dark, and beautiful like our dad. I'm short, blond, and almost as adorable as our mom."

"I see."

"Allison is Bailey's manager. She'll jump in and help you, too."

"Becca, I know you mean well, and I meant it when I said I'd stick around for a couple days, but you do know that any investigation needs to be conducted by officers of the law only?"

"Mostly."

Harry laughed.

I smiled up at his friendly eyes, which were now shaded by the brim of his hat. "I mean, of course, I know that, but like I said, I'll look for ways that Peyton is innocent. It's the least I can do for a family member. She was such a sweet kid, Harry. Really she was."

Harry nodded doubtfully and adjusted the hat.

"What do you think of South Carolina?" I said as I swung my attention back to the other side of the lot.

"It's much greener than Arizona, but most places are, and it's got lots more humidity. The parts I've seen are beautiful, but I haven't seen very much. I came straight to Bailey's."

I was about to offer a tour, but the first food truck rumbled into the parking lot, making sightseeing much less important.

"Paco's Tacos," Harry said as he read the side panel. "Sounds good."

"It does," I said. The name of the truck was painted across the yellow side panel in black letters that were framed by a red whimsical scribble and pictures of bow tie confetti in a rainbow of colors. There were no pictures of tacos, or any other kinds of Mexican food fare, but the design did its job of bringing attention to the truck and somehow making the idea of eating tacos sound like a good one, or at least a fun, festive one.

Only a couple seconds later another truck pulled in. This one's side panel had a number of animated chickens painted onto a white background. The chickens were cartoonish as well as chock full o' personality, with big smiles and winks and thumbs-up (okay, wings-up). The name painted along the top of the panel was simply "Wings."

"That sounds good, too," Harry said.

"Maybe we should have had more than coffee at Maytabee's," I said.

"Maybe." Harry laughed.

Allison and Sam directed traffic well, but when I noticed that both Ian and Brenton, the homemade dog biscuit guy, were assisting, I felt like I was neglecting an unspoken duty.

"I should go help," I told Harry. "Wanna come? It'd be a good way for you to meet Sam and some of the other people from the market."

He looked toward the crowd and frowned.

"Do you think Peyton will recognize you?" I said.

"Absolutely," he said. "And I'm not sure I want her to see me yet. I'll just stick back here a bit."

"Sounds good. After everyone is settled, I'll grab Sam and come find you. Or we'll connect this evening. I don't know how long any of this is going to take."

"You still have my cell?" Harry asked.

We confirmed that we still had each other's numbers. We'd shared them before I left Arizona. As we looked at our phones, I realized that back then I'd thought I would probably never dial Harry's number. Though I didn't like the reason he was in South Carolina, it was good to see him. It would be even better to see him if Peyton turned out to be innocent of the things he thought she'd done.

I hurried across the parking lot and joined the others just as the third truck arrived. This one was a cupcake truck. It was painted with soft pastel colors and giant but realistic pictures of cupcakes that made my mouth water. How was I supposed to stay inside the market at my stall and sell my jams, jellies, and preserves when all this delicious food was going to be a mere parking lot away?

I watched as Sam and Allison directed traffic, pointing the trucks to their spots, which were simply spaces along the outside edge of the parking lot, beside a curb that bordered the open patch of land I'd seen them inspecting earlier.

The land was not used for anything and wasn't taken care of. It was about twenty by thirty yards of ignored grass and weeds. I wondered if Sam and Allison had been discussing whether it was too ugly for the truck vendors to have to look at or so ugly that having them parked next to it would hide it from market customers for a couple weeks, at least.

I didn't have time to ask. Allison saw me and immediately asked me to welcome the cupcake truck baker.

The truck was called "Caked It" and the driver, owner, and baker of the business inside was Bushu Bonuhun. She'd come to Monson from the not far away Greenville, South Carolina. She was tall, thin, and wide shouldered; pretty, with sharp facial features that made her look more delicate than her height and shoulders.

"Welcome to Monson," I said.

"Thank you, darlin'," she said, her accent heavy and her voice surprisingly deep, as she extended a hand. She had a firm grip and a forceful shake. "I've been here a time or two over the years. Love this market, and I was excited when they told me this was where I was going to park for a bit."

"We're happy to have you here. What can we do to make your time easier?"

"Get up at about three in the morning and get my batters started." She laughed.

"Do I get to lick the spoons and bowls?" I said.

"We might be able to work something out."

For a few minutes we were a flurry of movement, Basha and I. I helped her make sure the truck was level and parked where Allison wanted it to be parked, which was at the front of the line and closest to the market entrance. Basha invited me inside for a quick tour. We went through a door that was on the side of the truck facing the patch of land. Once inside, Basha opened the awning over the serving counter, which was part of the panel that faced the parking lot.

I was struck by not only the cozy size of the work and preparation spaces, but also by the efficiency that was necessary to go along with the limited space. While standing mostly in place, Basha pointed out the preparation table that held a fancy mixer and shelves that held her cupcake tins when they were empty or filled with batter or finished cupcakes. Two squat refrigerators were along the back, and two stacked ovens were to the side of the counter space. Dishes, bowls, and other utensils all had designated spots. There was a place for everything, and everything had to be in its place or a mess would surely ensue.

I tried to imagine making my jams and jellies in such tight quarters, and the idea made me claustrophobic. I could probably manage it given enough time and trial, but I'd grown accustomed to my big kitchen and I wasn't ready to trade it in for a truck.

I learned that the reason for lining the trucks up next to the patch of land wasn't to hide it, but to hide something else instead: generators. All the trucks needed either access to electricity or a place to put a power generator. Bailey's made power available to the vendors inside the market, but since there'd been little to no time to prepare for the trucks' arrival, Allison hadn't managed to get power out to the parking lot. Generators would have to do for a day or two at least.

The activity level increased even more when the fourth truck arrived. Hank was big and burly, with bright blue eyes and short brown hair. He sold bowls of homemade ramen noodles topped or mixed with all kinds of things. I had no idea you could do so much with ramen. His truck was simply called "Noodle Bowls," and his side panels were painted with some of the items he put in the bowls along with the noodles. The pictures of meats, vegetables, and spices were just as appealing as Basha's cupcakes, but in a different way, of course.

Hank had a big voice and a big laugh, and was good-natured about the lack of electricity and the need for the generators, even though I could see he didn't want to be. I wondered if he would complain to Allison in private. I hoped not.

Between burly Hank; Daryl, the wing man (he liked referring to himself that way); Mel, the Paco in Paco's Tacos (he explained that Mel's Tacos just didn't have an authentic ring to it); Basha; and those of us from the market, it wasn't long before all but one of the trucks were lined up in their appropriate spots and ready to prepare and sell food.

Daryl reminded me more of an absentminded professor than a "wing man." He was tall with red bushy hair and glasses that didn't seem to fit right on his nose; they were off-kilter every time I looked at him, but he didn't seem to care. Other than sharing his nickname, he didn't have much to say, but his smile was friendly enough when he was in close proximity to other conversations. He moved slowly but efficiently. I saw him stretch his back a time or two and I hoped he wasn't overexerting himself.

Mel was the youngest of the group, so far. He was about twenty-five and seemed more surfer dude than taco chef. His blond hair and tanned skin made me wonder if he typically parked his truck on a beach somewhere, but I had to file away my curiosity for later. He spent most of his time helping other people with their trucks, lending a hand wherever he was needed. We'd finished with most of the manual labor and I was about to strike up a conversation when the fifth truck turned into the parking lot.

I stepped away from Mel and searched for Allison. She'd separated herself from everyone else as she jogged toward the approaching truck. I hurried to catch up to her.

"I guess we'll know if that's her soon enough," Allison said when she noticed me.

It was a bright yellow truck with happy black letters that said "Gourmet Hot Dogs." There were no food pictures, no list of toppings. Just a giant painted spatula that angled down and around the word "Dogs." It was simple but, surprisingly, not boring.

The young woman behind the wheel sent Allison and me a huge smile as she steered to the spot that Allison pointed her toward. There was no question that it was our cousin.

Once the truck stopped, she bounded out of it and ran to us.

"Allison, Becca, it's so great to see you. Are you surprised?"

As hugs were given all around, Allison and I both said

things like "Yes!" and "Very!" and "How did this all come together?"

"It was really just by accident," Peyton said breathlessly. "I was surfing the Net and I saw something about a food truck promotion program where they were sending food trucks all over the country this summer. They mentioned that some of the locations were farmers' markets. I called them and asked if I could be involved and then asked to come to Bailey's. It was a great reason to come see family, mostly you two. I hope you're not mad I didn't let you know I was coming." Peyton was all smiles and prettiness. She'd always been pretty, but I thought she must have hit a whole new stride in her twenties. She'd become beautiful.

"You drove all the way from Arizona?" I said.

Peyton blinked. "I did! Cool, huh?"

"Very," Allison said.

"It was a long trip, but the truck did just fine. I'm so glad to be here!"

"Excuse me, ladies. Allison, there's a gentleman from the bank and another one from the city business office here to see you. I hate to interrupt but they seem impatient." Ian smiled at me and Peyton after he spoke to Allison.

"Thanks, Ian," Allison said as she looked over his shoulder. "I'll be right there."

"Ian? You're Becca's Ian? Of course you are. You're exotic and handsome and have a ponytail and"—Peyton stepped next to him and lifted a sleeve of his T-shirt—"tattoos. Yep, you must be *the* Ian. I've heard such good things about you. I'm Peyton, Becca and Allison's cousin."

Ian smiled pleasantly at Peyton and me again as they

shook hands. "Nice to meet you, Peyton. Excuse me. Duty calls," he said before he turned and walked with Allison back to the growing group by the other trucks.

"Yep, that was Ian, and he is amazing and wonderful, and he and I aren't dating any longer," I said to Peyton. "But we're very good friends."

Sam was helping Hank with something near the front tire of the noodle truck. He wasn't far away and I could have pointed him out, but it seemed like too casual a way to let Peyton know about the new guy in my life.

"Oh. Oh, dear. I'm sorry. The last I'd heard was that you were together," Peyton said.

"It's okay," I said.

"I'm sorry," Peyton said again. But this time she didn't sound chastised. She sounded baffled. "What in the name of strawberry jam and jelly is wrong with you, cuz? He's . . . a lot to take in, I think."

I laughed. "He's all you think he is, Peyton, but I'm afraid we weren't meant to be. Later I'll introduce you to the man I think really is the one. For now, what can we do to get you set up? Looks like you'll be last in the line."

"Not much. It's too late to cook much of anything today, but I'll spend some time prepping for tomorrow."

"Let me get you hooked up with your generator," I said.

"Sounds great."

I looked across the parking lot at Harry. It was as if he hadn't moved an inch from his stoic pose against the car. I was pretty sure he saw me looking. The cowboy hat tipped ever so slightly. I decided not to wave, but I tried to smile quickly without Peyton noticing before we stepped around the truck to get the generator hooked up.

We weren't there long and I hadn't had a chance ask about anything, including her life in Arizona, before Allison poked her head around.

"Could use your help, Becca," she said.

"I'll take over." Mel from the taco truck strode toward me and Peyton and the generator. He might have looked like a surfer dude, but he was a hard worker. However, anyone who owned a food truck would have to have a strong work ethic, wouldn't they? Like farmers' market vendors, most of the work was done by one person.

"Thanks," I said as we crossed paths and I joined Allison.

"Come with me to talk to these men," Allison said. "The guy from the bank has been bugging me for weeks about coming to talk to the vendors regarding some ideas he has. I could use your moral support and, frankly, your bluntness if we need to get him off the subject. I don't like to make any decisions for the vendors without their viewpoint in mind. Don't be shy about sharing your opinion or whatever you think the other vendors' opinions might be."

"Glad to help," I said.

The two men we approached stood out from everyone else. They looked nothing like market workers, or food truck chefs. They were both in dress pants, dress shirts, and ties. I couldn't imagine how miserable they were in the heat. I was empathetically relieved that they didn't wear jackets, too.

I glanced quickly back and across the parking lot again. Harry still hadn't moved at all as far as I could tell.

I gave my full attention to Allison. I was honored to be her "bad guy" if I needed to be. She rarely asked for or needed my help. She was so darn good at everything. It was always great to be Allison. I liked it when I had a rare moment or two of it being great to be me.

Three

I wasn't given an opportunity to display my "blunt" skills.

Though Mr. Lyle Manner and Mr. Robert Ship were nice enough, they were also very formal. I wasn't used to formal and it made me uncomfortable. Allison introduced them specifically as Mr. Lyle Manner and Mr. Robert Ship, and they didn't ask that we call them by their first names, so we didn't.

Mr. Manner was from a local branch of the American Investors Bank and Trust. He was tall, very thin, with a pointy chin and short, perfectly smooth gray hair. His gray pants were a shade lighter than his hair, and his red tie made a bold statement against all the gray. He reminded me of a photographic special effect that turned the entire world black and white and shades of gray except for a few splashes of red here and there.

Mr. Ship was from the Monson City Business Licensing Division, or MBD for short. He was just barely taller than me and round, with a totally bald head and the most adorable nose I'd ever seen. I wondered if he thought lots of people were cross-eyed because of where their eyes landed when they were talking to him, right on his nose.

"Ms. Reynolds," the tall Mr. Manner said to Allison as he looked down at her and she looked up at him, "I understand you don't feel like you should interfere with your vendors' bank account decisions, but I assure you, having them all bank at one place, one bank, will make their lives much easier."

"Please call me Allison. And I appreciate what you're saying, but I think you might misunderstand how we do things here. There is no account sharing, Mr. Manner. Each vendor does their own thing. They are individual stall owner/operators. There's no benefit to them to all bank at the same place because they each have their own accounts, chosen for their own reasons. Perhaps they bank close to their homes, or along the routes they travel. They have to do what's best for them, individually."

They didn't know Allison nearly as well as I did, of course, so they probably didn't hear the incredulity in her voice. To her credit, she was toning it down, but I knew what was causing it. How could someone in the banking industry not understand that farmers' market vendors were individual owner/operators? Everyone was in charge of their own products and their own money. Frankly, it was one of the benefits of working at the market. Bailey's offered us a location, but we still got to have our own businesses.

"All right. Well, here's a proposal. What if we remove all banking fees for the Bailey's Farmers' Market main account if at least twenty of your vendors move their accounts to our bank?"

"Oh," Allison said. Again, she tried to hide it, but I could hear her disbelief, even with just one word. The "deal" felt more like bribery than a business offer. "Well, I'm not sure I'm the person you should talk to about that. I'll pass it along to the market owners, or you are welcome to talk to them yourself."

"Did I hear you say you're a local banker?" Peyton appeared behind my shoulder.

"Yes, ma'am. Mr. Lyle Manner, at your service," he said as he extended a hand.

"Peyton Chase. I'm from Arizona and there's no branch of my bank here locally. I'm thinking about sticking around South Carolina for a little while and I should probably set up an account."

"At your service," Mr. Manner repeated. "Shall we schedule an appointment?"

"You'll need a local, temporary business license, too, Ms. Chase," the shorter, rounder Mr. Ship added with what felt like a rude interruption. "In fact, that's what I'm here to talk to you about, Ms. Reynolds. Well, I'm here to help get the food truck temporary licenses set up, but it also seems that some of your market vendors are lacking a proper permanent business license. We need to get that remedied."

"Allison. Please. We require all the vendors to post their

licenses, Mr. Ship. We also require them to give us a copy for our files. I'm not aware of any unlicensed vendors. Do you know the specific vendors I need to talk to?"

"Yes, I have their names." Mr. Ship opened a pristine leather binder he'd been holding and lifted a single page from the top of a short stack of papers inside. "Here."

Allison took the paper. "Two vendors?"

"Yes."

"That's not too bad, but there might be a mistake. Betsy is always on top of everything. And Jeff Kitner . . . well, he has a cart, but I'm pretty sure he has a business license, too. I'm happy to follow up on these right away," Allison said.

"That would be very helpful." Mr. Ship turned back to Peyton, handing her a piece of paper, too. "Fill this out. I can pick it up tomorrow morning, get it expedited, and have everything in place quickly." He turned back to Allison. "I can do that for all of the food truck vendors."

"Thank you," Allison said.

"That would be great. Thanks," Peyton said. Something in her tone caused me to look more closely at her. It wasn't that she wasn't agreeable, but like Allison, there was something underneath the words, perhaps something contradictory. But as I inspected her, all I saw were her slightly crossed eyes focused on Mr. Ship's nose.

"I'll be by first thing in the morning, but here's my card if you have questions." He handed Peyton one of his cards.

"Thanks again," she said before she turned to the banker. "Mr. Manner, can we talk over there, in private? I don't really mind Becca and Allison knowing my financial circumstances, but I don't want to make anyone uncomfortable."

"Of course, of course," Mr. Manner said.

Peyton smiled at Allison and me and then went with Mr. Manner to a spot deeper into the parking lot where the only other people who could have heard them would have had to be inside the old parked Jeep that they stood next to. I didn't think anyone was inside the Jeep, but looking that direction gave my eyes a chance to seek out Harry again. He was still there, still in statue mode.

Mr. Ship cleared his throat. "I'll stop by and talk to each food truck vendor, Ms. Reynolds, if that's okay, and let them know we can expedite things quickly."

"Of course," Allison said. "Thank you."

"And please check on the delinquent licenses as soon as possible."

"Right away."

Mr. Ship smiled professionally and stepped around us to make his way toward the other trucks. It was as I watched him that I noticed Mel, Hank, and Daryl grouped together outside the taco truck. They were looking toward Peyton and Mr. Manner still out by the Jeep.

I realized that Mel probably hadn't just wanted to be helpful to Peyton. Perhaps he and the other two men thought she was cute. Frankly, they'd be blind not to notice her. She was more than cute; she was stunning.

I sent the three men a critical squint. She might be mostly a grown-up, and she might potentially be in trouble with the law, but Peyton was still my cousin and they'd better be polite and respectful. They didn't notice me.

"You think Peyton can handle whatever needs to be handled?" I said, mostly meaning the business dealings with

Mr. Manner and Mr. Ship, but covertly meaning the three men whom Allison hadn't noticed. "I still think of her as our little cousin who needs protection and guidance."

Allison laughed. "We taught her how to jump off the rope swing at just the right spot so she wouldn't hit rocks in the lake. I believe you taught her how fun it was to tie a bunch of firecrackers together and light them off at once. I'm not sure we were the best examples."

"Ah, the good old days," I said.

"She'll be fine," Allison said before she glanced unhappily at the time on her phone and then at the trucks that still needed her attention.

Now wasn't a good time to let Allison know about Peyton's potential legal issues, but she needed to know as soon as possible. Later would have to work, though. Allison currently had enough on her plate.

"Hey, why don't I talk to Betsy and Jeff about their licenses?" I offered. "I know, I know, it's not my job, but it's not a big deal. I can handle it. I know them both well enough. I will explain how busy you are. They won't care."

"I'm not sure, Becca," Allison said. "It's an official conversation; it should come from the market manager."

"Those two won't care, I promise."

She didn't take long to think about it.

"All right," she said. "But if there are any issues, call me immediately."

"I will."

"Thanks, Becca," she said as she hurried away.

I also wanted to tell her about Harry, but later would be

better for that, too. I looked across the parking lot again, expecting to find him still there. But he wasn't. He and his small car were gone.

Peyton and Mr. Manner were deep in conversation, presumably about her bank account. I did a double take at them when I realized that something had changed. Neither of them seemed happy. Peyton's arms were crossed in front of her and Mr. Manner seemed to be speaking sternly to her, or was that just their height difference and my perception? I took a step toward them, thinking I might need to intervene.

But Allison's words rang in my mind. I hoped Peyton really was okay. The fact that Harry had chased her from Arizona meant she might not be, but I didn't know how to jump into her current conversation without seeming like I was doing anything other than interfering.

Harry had said he didn't have any solid evidence or she would have been arrested by now. Maybe she was totally innocent; maybe he wouldn't find any solid evidence. I hoped not.

As I turned again to make my way into the market, I caught Sam's eye. He smiled and winked quickly before he crouched beside the noodle truck tire again. Oh, how I liked his smiles and winks.

I shook off the flirtation. I was over thirty and twice divorced. Giddy, girly stuff was reserved for younger, less jaded women who weren't responsible business owners and who hadn't just agreed to perform an important task for the market manager.

I couldn't help it, though. I liked the things his smiles did to me. I often wondered at what point this would all stop. When would we become either tired as heck of each other or so used to each other that boredom set in? No matter—I hoped we both hung in there long enough to find out.

I wove my way through the parking lot and then down the first aisle to the left inside Bailey's entrance. Betsy was still in her stall, but that wasn't a surprise; she typically stayed at the market through the entire afternoon. There were still a few tomatoes for sale in her bins, and she'd sell them all before she left. Though we didn't know each other well or deeply, she and I had always gotten along. She was the first one to introduce me to tomatoes topped with peanut butter. The discovery had been one of the best and most surprising culinary snack moments of my life, and had cemented my admiration for the earthy woman who had a way with her produce that brought people from all over the state to her stand.

Last summer, she created a red pasta sauce that had been both a blessing and a curse to her business. It was (not surprisingly) delicious, which meant that even more people traveled to Bailey's from far and wide to purchase a bottle of Betsy's Best and Bodacious. It tasted exactly as described. It was by far the best pasta sauce I'd ever eaten and its tangy, yet subtly sweet flavor, was, indeed, bodacious. She'd had so many customers and orders this summer that about a month earlier she'd asked to use my kitchen, which gave her much more room to work than her own kitchen. Betsy and I had figured out a schedule where she and I could both use the kitchen for our products but not be in each other's way.

She'd offered to pay me, but I'd traded the time in the kitchen for a few jars of sauce, with more jars whenever I wanted them. I didn't intend to take advantage of the offer, but I sure liked the sauce.

Her current sauce inventory was down to one bottle. She sat on a folding chair in her stall, her long brown hair pulled back into a neat ponytail, her beautiful makeup-free ivory skin shining but not in a sweaty way. Allison was like that; she could work hard and not break a sweat or mess up her hair. I took one box from my truck to my stall and my short hair looked like it could use a comb, and depending on the temperature, my cheeks were ruddy with either heat or cold.

"Hey, Betsy," I said as I approached her stall.

"Becca! It's great to see you. Perfect timing. I have one bottle left." She stood and reached for the sauce.

"I still have a bottle, but I have no doubt that the second it is gone, I'll be back for more."

"Sounds good. What's up?"

"You know about the food trucks?" I said.

"Sure. I already have a couple orders for tomatoes. Some tall, quiet professor type and a kid that might still have sand in his sun-streaked hair." She laughed.

"I know exactly who you're talking about. All five of the trucks are out in the parking lot now. Allison's there, too." I eyed the business license that was posted on the back pole of her stall. It was in the same spot I put mine in. "Anyway, a couple of the businesspeople from downtown are out there. One is from the bank, but the other one is from the city offices . . ."

Betsy's face soured and she threw one hand up to a hip. "Let me guess: Robert Ship is out there and he's complaining that I don't have a current license."

"Yes. How did you know?"

"Robert has been a thorn in my side for three weeks now." She turned and stepped surely to the license and pulled it off the pole. "Is he still out there?"

"I'm not sure."

"Would you mind watching my stall for just a second? I'll run out and talk to him. His records are messed up apparently. We've played phone tag, leaving increasingly impatient messages for each other. I even went into the office personally to try to take care of it," she said with much more anger than I thought she would display over a simple misunderstanding.

I'd never seen Betsy as worked up as she was at that moment. Even when her customer lines stretched down the aisle, she kept her cool. Her pretty ivory cheeks were suddenly dotted with pink.

"You do have a second, don't you?" she said.

"I do. Go on." I'd told Allison I would talk to Jeff, too, but there was no way I could leave now.

Betsy marched down the aisle, her long bohemian skirt flapping backward as she moved, reminding me of a witch with a spell and a specific Muggle in mind. I didn't want to be on the other end of that wand.

I moved to the spot behind her front table and took in the view. It was always interesting to see the market from a different stall's perspective, and this was the first time I'd been on this side of Betsy's table. I could see Abner's and

Ian's stalls much better from this vantage point. Ian's stall was empty, but I knew he was out helping with the trucks.

Abner, the wildflower man, was organizing a small bouquet, his arms moving precisely and quickly, his old fingers still nimble and able to gather, arrange, and then tie a piece of string around a group of stems in record time.

The bouquet in progress was for a man who was just the right age to make me wonder if he was buying it for a romantic partner, his mother, or his daughter. It was fun to spend a moment pondering where the colorful flowers would go once they left Bailey's.

"Is this for sale?" A woman pointed at the remaining bottle of sauce. She was tall and very thin with short gray hair but an unwrinkled youthful face.

"Yes, it is," I said.

"I'll take it," she said as she reached into her giant woven bag.

She handed me a twenty. I hadn't asked Betsy where she kept her cash box, but it was easy to find, on a small table in the back corner of the stall. I kept hold of the twenty, but pulled out the change for the customer. Once I gave her the change, I took the twenty back to the cash box. I hadn't put it away immediately, because I wasn't sure how Betsy organized her money and I didn't want to make the customer wait a couple seconds for me to learn the system. If Betsy did things the way I did, anything bigger than a ten would go under the tray, tens and smaller bills up top in the compartments.

There were no twenties in the top tray, so I figured Betsy worked the same way I did and I would find twenties underneath. The second I lifted the tray, though, I knew I should have probably just left the twenty on top and let Betsy sort it out.

There were some larger bills under the tray: three twenties and one fifty. But there were other things, too. I wished I hadn't noticed them but they were impossible to ignore. Two trifolded pieces of paper were under the bills. They were arranged so that I could see big, bold stamped letters on each of them. One said "OVERDUE" and the other said "DELIN-QUENT." It was also impossible to ignore the letterhead next to each of the stamped notices. The two letters were from American Investors Bank and Trust, the bank where Mr. Lyle Manner, the man who'd I'd thought might be reprimanding my cousin a few minutes earlier, worked.

After the information that I should never have seen was burned onto my brain, I dropped the twenty into the cash box and put the tray back in place. Betsy might not even think about what bill the last customer had used. She might never suspect that I'd seen what I'd seen. I wasn't going to tell her.

I hadn't really seen anything anyway. I hadn't unfolded and read the letters. They could have been . . . well, they could have been a misunderstanding of some sort, or not Betsy's. None of my business.

I wondered if she was unpleasantly surprised to see a representative from American Investors Bank and Trust out in the parking lot along with Mr. Ship.

Also none of my business.

As could happen, market traffic suddenly dwindled to almost nothing, with only a few customers left roaming the aisles. It was a typical late afternoon weekday crowd. Allison had mentioned that the market managers were thinking about opening late on a weekday other than Friday, but until that happened, the late afternoon would remain the best time for vendors who didn't want to pack up yet to grab a nap or catch up on a good book. I didn't think I should leave until Betsy came back so I grabbed the gossip magazine that was sitting on another chair and opened the cover.

"Becca." A voice that sounded angry grabbed my attention before I could turn another page.

"Hi, Jeannine," I said as I put the magazine down and popped up to attention.

Jeannine Baker was one of the market's egg vendors. Her eggs were the freshest, best eggs I'd ever tasted. Jeannine was loyal to Bailey's and never missed a day at her stall, but she was also one of Allison's more challenging vendors. Jeannine was suspicious of everyone and everything. The world was against her, she was sure.

"Becca," she repeated, making my name somehow sound like one syllable. "What is with the trucks?"

"They'll just be here a couple weeks, Jeannine, and I bet they buy eggs from you," I said, hoping I'd answered correctly.

"Will the market managers want us all to get trucks?" Jeannine was small and thin, with short hair and stern, sharp features. I often wondered if she'd been born that way or if she'd transformed over the years.

"No—not at all, Jeannine. They might like the trucks, but they'll never get rid of the stalls," I said. The idea hadn't occurred to me; most of Jeannine's ideas never occurred to me until she mentioned them. She had a way of planting unexpected seeds.

"I hope not. I don't know about all these newfangled changes," Jeannine said.

"Newfangled?" There wasn't any way to be less newfangled than we were at Bailey's. We still had our individual stalls made with tent canvas. The parking lot was paved, but the market floor was simply the dirt ground. The Smithfield market a half an hour away was slightly more newfangled than we were with an aluminum top over the canvas tents.

"Yes, like the misters. We worked here for years without any such thing. Now we have misters. Trucks might be right around the corner," Jeannine said.

I wanted to laugh, but I didn't even crack a smile because I wouldn't want to offend my paranoid friend and co-vendor.

"We'll be okay, Jeannine. I promise we won't have to get trucks."

"I hope you're right."

"I am."

"Hello, Jeannine," Betsy said from over Jeannine's shoulder.

"Betsy, what do you think of all this truck activity?" Jeannine asked.

"I think it's great," Betsy said, but her tone didn't sound great. Instead, she sounded defeated—or as though she was working at not sounding defeated but couldn't quite get there. I inspected her face closely. She had her emotions under control, but there was a small twitch at her left eye. Maybe it was nothing, but I doubted it.

"You do?" Jeannine said.

"Sure. I bet some of them buy eggs from you. They'll be

gone in few weeks. They're trucks, they're not meant to be parked for long. It's just a fun promotion for them and for the market. But the nature of their businesses means they're on the road, always going someplace."

"Oh, I know, but I bet they get so much business at Bailey's that they stick around, and I'm just having a hard time thinking it's a good plan, even if they do buy eggs from me."

There was no sense in arguing with Jeannine when her mind took hold of an idea. Betsy just smiled patiently at her and said some of the same words I had.

"It'll be okay, Jeannine."

"I hope so."

With that final declaration, Jeannine sniffed once, turned, and moved purposefully back to her own stall.

"Even with all that, she really is a likable person," Betsy said.

"Yes, she is. Maybe it's just that she's one of us, you know?"

"I do. That makes sense." Betsy took a deep breath and then let it out slowly as she looked down the aisle in the wake of Jeannine's departure.

"You okay?" I asked.

"Oh." She looked at me and forced a small smile. "All is well. I didn't get the misunderstanding cleared up, but I will. I'm sure."

"Your last bottle sold," I said cheerfully.

"That's great. Thanks, Becca. I know you have your own stuff to do, but I appreciate your help."

"No problem at all. I'm packed up for the day," I said.

"Yes. Fortunately, I'm a little ahead of the game. My inventory is good for another week. I won't have to work this evening."

"That must be nice." I said, just to continue the conversation. In fact, I was frequently ahead of schedule and was this week, too. It was a good feeling.

Betsy nodded absently.

"Can I help you load up or anything?" I said.

"No, I'm good," she said, a little more pep in her voice. "Thanks again, Becca."

"My pleasure."

Betsy stepped around the table, making her way into the stall. Unless I wanted to crowd the small space, my only real option was to go the opposite direction.

I stood in the aisle a moment, but she moved directly to the bins and started moving the remaining tomatoes to a small box that had been stored underneath. Even packing up the tomatoes proved she was off. She was always at the market until it closed if she wasn't sold out.

"See you later," I said.

"Later, Becca," she said as she continued to load.

I turned and walked slowly away, my mind on Betsy more than my next task, talking to Jeff. I'd never once known her to be anything but her level self, friendly but not gushy, smart but kind of silly sometimes, earthy. She ate more vegetables than anything else, but I knew she loved cookie dough ice cream with a deep passion. She was what my grandmother would have described as a lovely person.

Which meant nothing when it came to the items I'd seen

in her cash box. And she'd acted funny when she came back to her stall.

As I reached the aisle intersection, I stopped and laughed at myself. Why was I turning this into a mystery? Why was I making this more important than it probably was? I'd check on Betsy tomorrow and make sure she was okay, but even earthy, happy, level people are allowed less than cheerful moments.

"What's so funny?"

I turned to find that Ian's stall wasn't empty after all. Or at least it wasn't empty now. Ian was there, sitting in a chair toward the back, which was open to the load/unload area on the inside of the U-shaped market. The back flap was pulled up to make room for a tall piece of yard art that he was assembling.

"Hey, Ian. I'm overthinking something," I said as I stepped into his stall. There was no table in the front. In fact, he was barely in his stall anymore, and when he was, it was mostly so a customer could pick up a piece of art they'd ordered from him. Though he'd started at the market by making the yard art, his world had grown much bigger.

"You?" he said with a smile. "I can't imagine you over-thinking anything," he teased.

I smiled, too.

I liked the comfortable spot we'd found in our friendship and dating spectrum.

"That's a beautiful piece," I said as I crouched and lifted the end of one of the scoop-shaped wind catchers. From what I could tell, it looked like one wheel of scoops would go one direction and another wheel would go the other. The resulting illusion would be interesting. My boost up gave Ian the chance to use both hands to attach the top piece to the pole.

"Thanks, I'm pleased with it. I hope the customer is, too. There," he said. "Done. Couldn't have done it without you." He smiled.

We both straightened as he moved the piece to an upright position.

"You've only gotten better," I said. "A better artist. Your work was always great but it's improved."

Ian laughed. "I knew what you meant. Thanks. I don't do as many of these as I used to. I'm enjoying the farm, but once everything transitions into more a routine than just a bunch of work to get things started, I hope to do more yard art, too. It was my first passion."

If you looked up the word *artist* in the dictionary, there was a good chance Ian's picture would be next to the definition. He looked the part. But what wasn't obvious at first was his mathematically inclined mind. The calculations necessary to balance his sculptures required him to be good at math—really good. At first glance you'd have no idea he was so smart. At second glance, though, and once you'd had even a short conversation with him, you'd know he was not only exotic but intelligent, too.

"I hope you have the time. Farm going well?"

"Very well. If I stay on the right track, I will have giant and beautiful purple fields for many years to come."

"I bet it's amazing. How's George?" I asked. George had been Ian's landlord when he'd first moved to town. George had owned a big, old Tudor in the Ivy League district. Ian had enjoyed the apartment above the garage, and he and George had become close friends. When Ian purchased the land for the farm, he'd asked George to come along with him. George's eyesight had been progressively worsening, and the idea of leaving him alone in his big house didn't sit right. Fortunately, George did go with Ian and they and the black cat I had found when he was a kitten and given to George were getting along grandly, I hoped.

"He's doing very well. He's more help than I thought he would be. He loves working on the essential oils. He can go at his own pace. Between that, listening to audio books, and hanging out with Magic, his days are full and busy. I think he's happy. I'm sure he'd love for you to come out and visit. Sam, too."

"I will. Soon."

"So your cousin, the one with the truck?"

"Yeah. Sorry about the misunderstanding. We don't talk as much as we should."

"Oh. Not a problem. She and the guy from the business office were sure having a heated discussion out there. Allison had to break it up, and Betsy came over, too, and tried to help. Your sister had her hands full, but she handled it well," Ian said.

"Just a few minutes ago?" I said.

"Ten, fifteen," he said.

"I was watching Betsy's stall. She came back and seemed off—you know, funny. That's what I was overthinking just a second ago."

"Well, I think she was unhappy, too, but Peyton's problem was . . . a little louder, I guess."

"I'll ask Allison," I said. "How's your Betsy?"

Ian's Betsy had become his girlfriend shortly after I hadn't. She was a local young woman who operated a successful restaurant.

"She's fine. Leaving town for a while."

"Vacation?"

"Nope. Moving."

"What? How can she move? She owns the restaurant."

"Someone came in and offered her a bundle for it. She's heading up to New York and culinary school. She's going to come back when she's done and open a new restaurant."

Betsy was one of the hardest-working people I knew, but she'd taken a less than traditional path to restaurant ownership; she'd received an inheritance of sorts. She'd never had any sort of formal cooking or baking instruction and I knew she wished she had. Her hard work had gotten her far. It sounded like her ambition was still going strong.

"Wow, that's big. I'm sorry she's leaving for a while."

"It's okay. I like people to follow their dreams."

"You're good that way."

Ian smiled again.

I felt bad for him. I knew he liked her, but we hadn't discussed it that deeply. Our friendship still held clear memories of closer moments between us, and it would have been weird for us to go into detail about our new relationships. Ian and I would never date each other again, but we both respected what we'd had, and the evolution necessary to let it go completely.

Further conversation was interrupted by the arrival of Ian's customer, there to pick up his yard art. I got out of their way and started down the aisle again.

I was curious about Peyton and Betsy, not Ian's Betsy, but the one who sold tomatoes at the market. I'd ask Allison for more information about the altercations, but something had caused Betsy's blue mood. Maybe she felt like she missed a chance to talk to Mr. Ship because he'd been busy arguing with Peyton. And what would that have been about? Had Peyton argued with Mr. Manner—as I thought I'd seen—and then with Mr. Ship? Why? I hoped Allison had been paying attention.

For now, I picked up the pace. I still had a baked potato vendor to talk to.

Four

The potato cart had been placed at the end of the other aisle, the other leg of the U. I'd taken so much time at Betsy's and with Ian that there was a good chance that Jeff had packed up and gone home for the day, but he was still there, and still serving baked potatoes, even in the lingering late afternoon heat.

It was a clever idea. He baked the potatoes at home, wrapped in foil and in an oven like any good baked potato should be prepared. He kept the wrapped potatoes in the warming cubby belly of the cart. Just like with the food kept in airplane food carts, I was surprised by how many potatoes fit into the cubby. The toppings were housed in the refrigerated top of the cart, protected by a sneeze guard. Jeff set a table with plates, napkins, and utensils next to the cart. Since he was a stickler for food safety, I would be surprised if he truly was delinquent regarding his business license. Like Betsy, there had to be some misunderstanding.

Even with the heat of our summer days, customers loved his baked potatoes. And even with the odd time I'd approached the cart—in between lunch and dinner—I had to wait for two customers to get their orders before I could talk to him.

"Hey, Jeff," I said as the line and the utensils table cleared of customers.

"Becca, how's your day going?" Jeff said, his words cheerful, but his tone less so. He was a nice enough guy, but I always had a sense that he didn't really want to be nice, that he was thinking of less than nice things to say but keeping them to himself as he vocalized pleasant sentiments instead.

"Good. Yours?"

"Good. It sure is hot out, but it's been busy." Jeff's cart and table weren't located near any of the misters so he didn't know the crushing misery that hit most of us with the mechanical breakdown.

Jeff Kitner was young, maybe in his mid-thirties. He was handsome in a serious, angular way, with a sharp jaw and a sharp nose. He kept his wavy brown hair just long enough to be considered tousled. When he first started at the market, all the young, single women developed an almost constant craving for baked potatoes, but after a while his sour tone and personality made him and his food much less popular with the market vendors. His business had continued to thrive, but it became more about customers liking the potatoes, less about vendors trying to get a date.

He was from a small town in South Carolina. I couldn't ever remember the name of the town, but it was apparently smaller than Monson and had been an "okay" place to grow up, according to Jeff during the first and longest conversation he and I had ever had. I wondered if today's would be longer.

We'd gotten along okay. I liked his potatoes and he'd bought quite a few jars of my boysenberry jam—though as market vendors, we all subscribed to the idea that we didn't need to be each other's customers to be friends.

"I know." I fanned my hand in front of my face a couple times. "Hey, Jeff, I hate to bug you, but I'm helping Allison with some business details. She's out front working with the arriving food trucks and a bank and a town business office guy are out front with her. The business office guy works in the licensing division and he's gathering copies of all the market vendors' business licenses. He thought since he was here, it wouldn't hurt. I offered to do the legwork. Any chance I could get your license, make a quick copy, and bring it back to you?"

My story was a lie, and a weak one at that. But I'd decided to try it that way first. I didn't know Jeff well enough to single him out, and there was enough potential volatility about him that I didn't want to sound critical or combative. It might not have been the best idea I'd ever had; it didn't make much sense that the guy from the business licensing division would need copies of business licenses, because his office should already have them on file, but if Jeff wasn't listening closely, it might fly. I hoped he'd go along with it and he and I could be done quickly with our second longest conversation ever.

"Huh," Jeff said doubtfully. I continued to smile and look

him in the eye as the "bad" in my bad idea seemed to expand. "Well, I don't have a business license."

"Oh? Why not?" I said, genuinely surprised.

"Don't need one. And that guy you're talking about knows it. His name is Robert Ship, right?"

"I think so."

"Well, he's sent you to do some of his dirty work, Becca. I never have had a license because I don't need one. There's a clause in the law that says I don't. I've showed it to Mr. Ship a number of times. He can't find a way to validly argue that I'm wrong. He just keeps hounding me, but there's nothing legal to back him up. I'm sorry he thought you—or you and Allison—should continue the harassment. He shouldn't have done that."

No, he shouldn't have. If that was really what he'd done. I'd need more information to know for sure.

"But you are a retail establishment, right? You take money? Don't you have to report taxes? How do you do that and not be attached to a license?" My questions weren't meant to be accusatory. I was curious. My entire business, including my bank account, was tied to my license and my setup as a corporation.

"I'm self-employed, and since I have a cart, not technically a stall, I don't have to have a license. I have *food* inspectors inspect my cart to make sure I'm not breaking any *food* regulations, and I get clean inspections all the time. Look up the clause, number 458-098, in the county business regulations, and you'll see there's no requirement for me to have a license."

"Huh," I said, repeating Jeff's earlier exclamation. I wanted to point out that a business license wasn't a bad way to go anyway, and that setting his business up as a corporation of some sort was an even better way to protect himself, to keep clear of liability, to keep business and personal monies separate. But I didn't think I should lecture Jeff on the ins and outs of owning a business. If we'd been better friends, I might have, or if I didn't have a sense that *Jeff's way was the only way,* I might have. But I did have that sense. "Okay. I'll let Allison know."

"Thanks, Becca, and I'm really sorry he dragged you two into it." For the first time since I'd known Jeff, he actually sounded sincere. "I'll stop by his office and talk to him tomorrow morning and end this craziness once and for all. How's that?"

"Sounds great. And neither Allison nor I were inconvenienced." I smiled. "I might have just learned something new. Sorry to interrupt your day."

A young couple, each with an infant attached to their fronts in those things that I thought made babies look like turtles, approached the cart just as it seemed our conversation had reached an appropriate ending spot. I stepped back and observed Jeff a moment as he helped the customers. I didn't think what he'd said could possibly be correct, but I wanted to find out. I found a pen with a chewed cap in my short overalls' back pocket and scribbled the numbers 458-098 on the back of my hand before I made my way to the parking lot.

Surprisingly, Allison was easy to find this time. She hadn't left the parking lot, and I spotted her just as she emerged from the taco truck, her cell phone in her hand and a serious look on her face. She stepped a few feet back from the truck and turned to face it. Her hands had moved to her hips by the time I reached her.

"How's it going?" I said.

She looked around furtively and then leaned toward me. "Each truck has its own problem. No, I should call them challenges. Only one truck is ready to serve food. This one"—she nodded toward Paco's Tacos—"has a grill that doesn't heat evenly. I thought the bank guy and the business office guy were tough; they're nothing compared to the woman from the health department. She's something else. I understand her concerns, but she certainly has an abrupt style about her."

"Where is she?"

"Gone, but she'll be back tomorrow morning. Before then, we need to get the grill working, the refrigerator working better in the cupcake truck, all the barbeque sauce replaced in the wing truck, and all new cheese for Peyton's truck. The ramen truck is fine, I guess. So that's one out of five."

"My kitchen's available if anyone needs to cook or prep, and I know a couple electricians that might be able to help if we need them."

Allison smiled at me. "Got the electricians, but Mel and Daryl might want to use your kitchen. And Peyton could use some help shopping for cheese. I bet she'd enjoy the company."

"I can do that." I looked around. "Sam still around?"

"He's one of the electricians. He's in the cupcake truck."

"I didn't know he could do that stuff."

"Learn something new every day. Oh! How were Betsy and Jeff?"

"Okay. I need to follow up with them, but I have to ask

you a question about Jeff. He doesn't think he needs a business license. Sound familiar?" I said.

"I think I remember talking to him about that one time. I'll have to check my notes in his file." Allison frowned. "And Betsy was upset out here but I didn't get a chance to talk to her. I feel like I was remiss in my duties. I'm sorry, Becca, I shouldn't have bothered you with it."

"Don't be sorry. I like it when you think I'm responsible."

"You're very responsible," Allison said without even a small hint of sarcasm. She looked around again, not furtively this time, but curiously, assessing the situation. "If you're good to check with Mel and Daryl and then go with Peyton, I'd better follow up with Betsy and Jeff right away. I'll come back out here when I'm done."

"I can do that."

I decided that I wasn't sure if I was glad I was there to help, or if I wished I'd left earlier, before Harry arrived and my day took all these new turns.

I sighed and looked for Mel and Daryl. Fortunately, they were together, without Hank but in Hank's noodle truck, the only truck the health department had cleared. I spied them through the open counter window. They were facing each other, both with one hip leaning against the inside front counter. They were in the middle of a conversation that didn't seem either private or all that important so I approached.

"Hi, guys," I said.

"Hello." Both of their hips came off the counter and they turned to face me.

"I'm Becca." We'd all introduced ourselves earlier, but

considering the flurry of activity during the trucks' arrival, I decided it wouldn't hurt to refresh.

"Yeah, I'm Mel and this is Daryl."

"Right. Well, I know you have some truck issues. I have a big kitchen that's available if you need it for anything."

"That's very kind. Thank you. I'm fine. My issues will be resolved quickly," Daryl said with a frown as his arms crossed in front of his chest. It was impossible not to look at his glasses, noticing that they angled sharply down to the right. My fingers itched to straighten them.

Had I insulted him by mentioning the truck issues? I didn't think I had, but if so, he was far too sensitive.

"I think I'm all right, too," Mel said too cordially, his surfer hair swooping just right. He was compensating for Daryl's closed off body language. He leaned over the counter. "Does anyone else need any mechanical help? I'm good with generators." He winked.

I was caught off guard. Was he flirting? I didn't really think so, but the compensating had just moved to overcompensating.

"I'll ask my sister, the market manager," I said. "But thanks for all your patience today. We would have liked to have had your electrical hookups ready for you. Hopefully, that will be taken care of quickly."

Still leaning over the counter, Mel didn't miss a beat. He winked again and smiled extra big. "No problem. We can roll with it."

"So where's Hank?" I said.

Mel stood up. "Don't know. I was wondering that myself."

As if on cue, Hank appeared. He came out from between

Peyton's and Daryl's trucks. He looked flustered, but in a buff way. He shook his head and then ran his fingers through his hair before he noticed me watching him.

"Hey, buddy, what have you been doing?" Mel said to Hank. Mel's voice had changed from the friendly tone he'd tried to sell me to one that was laced with suspicion. He'd resumed leaning out of the counter window, but his smile was gone.

"Nothing, just checking on a couple of the generators," Hank said. He smiled at me. "Hello."

"The generators okay?" I said.

"Yeah, the generators okay?" Mel said.

Daryl had stepped backwards in the small space inside the noodle truck. His top half was cloaked in a shadow so I couldn't see the look on his face, but Mel's suspicion and Hank's somewhat discombobulated appearance made me wonder what they were all up to.

"It sounds like your kitchen is ready to go, but I was just offering mine to these guys. Offer goes for you, too. I have a big space if you need to use it," I said.

"I'm good. Thanks, though." He'd hurried past me and ignored Mel as he moved toward the front of his truck, stopping there as if to wait until it was polite to disappear again.

"Okay," I said. "Well, just let Allison know if you change your minds."

"We'll do that," Daryl said. He'd moved toward the counter again and out of the shadow. He was unquestionably uncomfortable about something, or he was naturally awkward.

I looked over the three men and decided that I didn't really need to know what they were up to. I still had some cheese shopping to do.

"See you later."

They all muttered similar sounding farewells.

I stepped toward Peyton's truck. Since it was last in line, it was closest to the parking lot's entrance and exit. It had front cab doors on each side, as well as small sliding doors behind the cab and on the box part of the truck. The sliding doors were obviously an afterthought, not part of the original truck but something that must have been added when the truck became a mini kitchen. I noticed that the other trucks had only one of these doors and it was on the side that didn't have the counter, the sides that were currently facing the empty plot of land. But Peyton's had two.

When I was about ten feet away from her truck, I noticed the sliding door on this side shut—it rebounded first like someone had pushed it too hard, but it stayed closed on the second try.

"Peyton," I said as I peered in through the tiny, foggy window at the top of the door. She must not have heard me as she moved toward the matching door on the other side.

It looked like she was carrying a small canvas bag and there was something about the way she held it tucked tightly under one arm that made me wonder if she was trying to hide it.

I stepped to the space between the front of Peyton's truck and the back of Daryl's. I moved slowly through the gap, craning my neck and hoping Peyton would come into view. I got to the other side just as the back sliding door opened and Peyton stepped out. She looked around and I pulled back, not wanting her to see me just yet. I leaned back out and watched as she took the bag from under her arm and held it in her hands. She stared at it a long time and then brushed off what looked like caked-on dirt. She muttered something to herself but no matter how much I strained to listen, I couldn't understand the words. She tucked the bag under her arm again and looked over the open plot of ignored land. She seemed to focus on one spot.

I looked in that direction and then back at her a few times. Was she looking at something specific or was she lost in thought, her eyes just happening to land where they'd landed?

Another few seconds later, she took a deep breath and let it out in what seemed to be a relieved sigh. She turned and disappeared back inside the truck. I went down into a crouch so she wouldn't see me through the front windshield.

I remained in the crouch for a few long seconds. Should I go see what she might have been looking at, or should I just knock on a sliding door and then escort her to the grocery store for some cheese? Finally, I threw caution to the wind and scurried out and toward the spot in the back.

The trek wasn't terrible, but the ground was uneven enough to slow down my scurry to a high-stepping jaunt. I stopped where I thought she'd been looking, and was surprised that there was something to see. The ground had been disturbed recently. The dirt was loose and too smooth, as if someone had dug there and then covered up the hole.

I went to my knees and used my hands to sift through the loose dirt. I didn't have to go too deep to determine that there was nothing to find except more dirt. Was it possible that Peyton had recently dug up the bag from this spot and this was the result?

I sat back on my heels and tried to understand what might be going on, what it might mean. Peyton could see me if she happened to step back out of the truck, and a part of me hoped she would. The moment would probably be uncomfortable, but might ultimately make it easier to ask her a slew of questions that had come to mind since Harry had arrived.

But then again, if she really had done illegal things in Arizona, my methods might only make it easier for Harry to catch her. I cringed. I really hoped she hadn't done something that would land her in trouble.

I stood and brushed off my knees before I hurried back to the truck, knocking on the back sliding door.

"Becca?" Peyton said when she opened the door. "You know there's another door on the other side? Next to the parking lot."

"I do, but this one seemed like the right one."

"Okay." She shrugged.

"I'm here to take you cheese shopping," I said.

"That would be very helpful. Thanks!"

"How about a quick tour before we go?" I stepped up and into the truck before she could stop me or hide the bag if it was sitting out.

"Of course," she said with no hesitation at all.

There was no immediate sign of the canvas bag, but I saw a few crumbles of dirt on the floor next to the doorway.

Similar to Basha, she stood in the middle of the truck and turned as she showed me the refrigerators, the grill, the storage shelves, and the other implements that made up her cooking space. It was efficient in ways that hadn't ever occurred to me until today. A few square inches made for a good spatula drawer. It was fascinating in an engineering way, but I had a hard time focusing on the places she wanted me to focus on as my eyes scanned for the canvas bag. However, she got my full attention when she opened one of the small refrigerators.

"What's that?" I asked as I pointed at a plastic-lidded container full of what looked like thick, dark ketchup. Even though Harry hadn't told me much more than there'd been a theft of a secret tomato recipe, I couldn't help but wonder if this might be resulting sauce.

"Oh, that's . . ." Peyton squinted in thought and frowned a moment. "That's a topping."

"For your hot dogs? What kind of topping?"

Peyton laughed. "Tomato. It's kind of amazing. I . . . well, I used to work for a restaurant that made something like it. This is my version and it's even better, or that's my opinion."

"You got their recipe?"

"Heavens no," Peyton said. "I figured out my own recipe, but I gotta tell you, Becca, they were none too happy when they tasted how close mine was to theirs."

"Uh-oh, did you get in trouble?"

Peyton looked at me a long moment as if she wanted to say more. Perhaps confide in me? I held my breath with the hope that whatever was on her mind (and whatever was in that canvas bag for that matter) would just pop out of her mouth and we could solve all the problems that needed to be solved.

But a second later she waved away the comment, closed

the fridge door, smiled her pretty smile, and said, "No, not at all. Come on, let's go shop for some cheese."

I scanned the compact kitchen one more time but there was no sign of the canvas bag. I watched as Peyton made sure every door to the truck as well as the panel over the serving counter was locked tight. Maybe she was just being smart and careful about the truck's security, but I thought I saw an extra intensity to her scrutiny.

Or maybe I was just reading too much into every single move she made.

Five

"I couldn't have just barged into her truck, Becca, you know that," Sam said with a smile.

We were sitting on a cushioned bench on my back patio, with Hobbit, my short-legged, long-footed, brown retriever mutt, lounging under us. I'd showered and was in clean short overalls and Sam had changed out of his uniform and into shorts and a T-shirt. His legs were stretched out in front of the bench and I had my legs over his. Though we were in the shade, we'd already gone through a pitcher of iced tea; the second pitcher, half-empty, glistened on the small table next to Sam.

Peyton and I had finished cheese shopping quickly. The one grocery store I took her to had everything she needed. I'd dropped off her with her cheese and then hurried home to Sam and Hobbit.

The sun hadn't set yet but it was well on its way. The western sky was painted with orange and yellow layers. Relaxing and cooling off might have been better accomplished inside, but our summer evening patio ritual was hard to break.

"I know, but what in the world could have been buried back there? How would Peyton have known about it? It's strange," I said.

"I think you should just ask her. She's your cousin, family. You can be blunt with family. In fact, I might have seen you be blunt a time or two with those who aren't family." Sam smiled at me over the rim of his glass as he took another sip.

He was tan this year. He'd been helping me with my strawberry and pumpkin plants as well as caring for the rest of my yard. He said he enjoyed the labor and I'd fully admitted to enjoying watching him work. In his police uniform you knew he was a pleasant enough looking guy, handsome and almost disturbingly observant with blue eyes which seemed to change shade with his mood or his thoughts. But when he wore civilian clothes and freed his wavy hair from the gunk and threw himself into physical labor, he was downright yummy. Visions of him moving in slow motion toward me as he swung a hoe over his shoulder had recently started filling my daydreams.

I told him as much not long ago and he'd laughed, mentioning that he wasn't quite "all that," but since I'd fallen under his spell, he was more than happy to think of himself as "yummy."

I knew without a doubt that it wasn't all about the way the tan looked on him; it was the attitude that had come with the tan. My house had, step-by-step, been turning into his house, too. He enjoyed the outside work as well as the inside work helping with my jams and preserves. The meaning of home had been changing for me as well. He'd become a bigger and bigger part of the definition, and his tanned skin and burnt-tipped nose were constant reminders of those welcome and happy changes.

However, I was still completely aware of the fact that I was twice-divorced, so maybe I wasn't very good with this sort of thing—the relationship thing. Counting on any of it working out might still be a bit premature.

He knew that about me, too, and had an uncanny knack for sensing when I might need a little space or was leaning toward a "freak-out" moment because everything seemed to be going too well, and that seemed so impossible considering my past experiences. He'd step back, maybe do something on his own outside, or perhaps head back into the police station for a little bit. The number of those moments had been decreasing, though. He knew it, but I wasn't sure if he knew I knew it.

Allison thought I was being both silly and stupid and I just needed to ask Sam to marry me. I kept telling her that a third marriage didn't bother me in the least, but a third divorce might just be too much to bear. She'd just shake her head and refrain from further comment.

"I could be blunt," I said. "I have no problem being blunt with Peyton, but there's more."

"What's that?"

"She's in trouble, Sam. Or might be. There's a police officer in town from Arizona. I met him when I was down there. He says she's suspected of assault, and theft of money and a secret recipe."

Sam set his glass on the table with the pitcher and looked at me with his serious eyes. "I think you'd better fill me in on some things."

"Me, too," I said.

I outlined the details regarding Harry and his reasons for traveling to South Carolina. Sam wasn't happy that Harry hadn't first contacted the local police department but was somewhat appeased when I told him that I'd called Harry on my way home and made plans for him and Sam to meet the next morning.

Sam made a few phone calls, including one to Harry to confirm the early morning meeting, and I managed to wrangle an invitation to attend.

However, after the calls, Sam said, "Becca, you might want to tell me about visiting police officers or potential legal issues only about a second or two after you learn about them. Not a few hours later."

I felt properly guilty. "I know. Sorry."

Sam smiled and shook his head. "You worry me, Becca, but you're pretty fun to have around so the worry is worth it, but still, be safe. Please."

I'd gotten a little better at being safe, about being a little less nosy, but he was right and I needed to improve. And even though he kept his tone light, I could hear the concern in his voice. There was no need for me to cause him unneeded worry, at least not about these sorts of things.

"I will, I promise," I said with a thoroughly brazen and flirtatious move to sit on his lap.

Neither of us spent much time worrying for the rest of the night.

Though you would think that the mere excitement about getting to attend a morning breakfast meeting with two police officers would be enough to render me wide awake, the caffeine boost from Maytabee's strongest ever in the universe blend was necessary. Sam had rescheduled the meeting for five o'clock—in the morning. When he awakened me at four thirty, I got up and ready with the most cheerful demeanor I could muster at such an early hour. It was rough.

Sam and Harry hit it off immediately. Well, in that way two serious men with serious matters to discuss can hit it off. They conversed easily and intelligently and before long were on the same page regarding Peyton and her potential crimes. I told Harry about the canvas bag, but was surprised by his reaction.

"You didn't see her pull it up out of the ground, right?" he said to me.

"No. I just saw her dusting it off."

"She might not have dug it up at all. The timing is questionable and might be off," he said.

"It seemed like a reasonable conclusion." As I said the words, I realized how right he was. I'd played a scene out in my head, but not all the pictures were real; I'd added a few. "Oh, I see. Should I just ask her about it? Tell her what I saw?"

Harry and Sam looked at each other.

"Not quite yet," Sam said, changing his mind from the night before. "Let me get a better feel for what's going on.

Harry and I can work together on this, Becca. Maybe you can talk to Peyton at some point about these things, but let's not let her think you're trying to catch her at something."

"Which is the opposite of what I'm doing. I'm going to prove that Peyton's innocent."

Sam put his hand over mine on the table. "We know she's family."

Harry nodded, but I sensed that Peyton being part of my family was the least of his worries.

Sam's radio buzzed. "Sam, you there?"

I recognized the voice as Officer Vivienne Norton's, the toughest female police officer in the entire county, maybe the state.

Sam reached to the handset that was secured to his shoulder. "I'm here, Vivienne. What's up?"

"Need you at the American Investors Bank and Trust. Immediately. You know where it is?"

"Sure. What's wrong?"

There was a slight hesitation before Vivienne spoke again. "Sam, we've got a 10-89."

Sam stood from the table. "At the bank?"

"Affirmative."

"I'll be right there. Gotta go," he said to no one and anyone who might be listening.

"Want me to come?" Harry asked.

"No, not right now. I'll get back with you later," Sam said. He looked at me like he'd just remembered I'd ridden with him. "Can you go with Harry?"

"Sure, but what is a 10-89?" I asked.

Sam hesitated. "Deceased person."

"Dead body?" I asked. "At the bank? Who?"

"I'm going to go find out. Go with Harry." Sam turned and hurried out of the coffee shop.

"This isn't good," I said as I looked at Harry.

"No, ma'am, these sorts of things are never good. But I'm sure Sam will take care of it."

"He will," I said as I looked out of Maytabee's front window. Who was dead? And how did they get that way?

And why was Peyton being in town now even more worrisome?

Six

Harry dropped me off at my house, and I took Hobbit out for her morning jog before loading up my truck with more jams and preserves and heading into Bailey's. I was like a teenager who couldn't stop checking her phone. No one called or texted, Sam included. Hobbit didn't appreciate that I seemed distracted, and by the time I told her I had to leave, she seemed relieved to get rid of me.

Harry said he'd probably see me back at the market later. We decided that I needed to introduce him to Allison as soon as possible. She needed to know what was going on with Peyton, too, and today would hopefully be less hectic than yesterday. But all those plans were tentative, depending upon what we learned about the events at the bank.

It was inappropriate, I knew, but I spent a brief moment being relieved that I hadn't been the one to find Monson's latest dead body. I'd been on that particular unlucky roll for some time. Maybe my luck was changing—I cringed at myself. I'd gone from inappropriate to wildly inappropriate.

I pulled into the load/unload area of Bailey's and parked the truck, realizing I'd been so distracted on the ride into town that I didn't remember the trip. I needed to get in the moment.

Other familiar trucks and vans were parked in their spots. Lots of others. I recognized most of them and realized the big turnout meant it was probably going to be a busy day at Bailey's. Most of the time a good majority of vendors worked from their stalls, but some days, when almost all the vendors were there, you knew a big crowd was expected. It looked like that was happening today, though I didn't know why.

My guess proved to be correct. I wasn't late, but the second I pulled open the back flap of my stall and started moving my inventory inside, I was met by the rumble of lots of eager customers.

Linda, my friend and stall neighbor, came out through her back flap just as I was grabbing the last box out of my truck.

"Becca, hey, you're earlier than normal, but I think that's a good thing. We're busy." She reached into the back of her van and pulled out a few pie boxes. Linda made and sold the best fruit pies in the history of all fruit pies. She dressed in a pioneer woman getup that only added to her *made by loving hands* reputation. "I ran a little behind this morning and I wonder if I'll ever catch up."

"What's the reason for the big crowd?" I asked.

"Your guess is as good as mine."

"You have any more pies in there?" I asked as I set the box of my preserves on the ground.

"No, these are my last few. We'll talk later," she said as she and her pie boxes slid through the gap in her back flap.

I retrieved the box of jams and with the same maneuver moved into my stall.

It didn't take long to get my product up and ready to sell. I had a couple customers, regulars, who swung by as I was stacking and arranging. They knew what they wanted and they had exact change so they were easy to take care of.

I'd built a good reputation too. Somehow I grew the most amazing strawberries, perfect for jams and preserves. I purchased other fruits (and peppers for my jalapeño mint jelly) from local growers and had become adept at making all kinds of delicious flavors. I gave the credit for the delicious strawberries to the South Carolina soil that I was lucky to have on my property. The recipes I used were from my Uncle Stanley, who'd purchased the land and house and had remodeled the barn into a kitchen with the idea of making jams and preserves as a retirement project. He and my aunt Ruth had been killed in a terrible car accident before he could make his first jar or see a strawberry plant produce even one piece of fruit. Allison and I had been their beneficiaries. I'd gotten the land, house, and recipes, and Allison had gotten some money, a comfortable amount that she'd put into a savings account to be used for her son Mathis's education.

I would always miss my aunt and uncle, their kind hearts and generous natures, but I knew they'd be pleased with the choices we'd made with their legacy.

As the flurry of business built even more, I happened to

see Betsy, the tomato lady, scurry down the aisle, seemingly in an agitated hurry. I might not have thought anything about it if I hadn't spent time with her the day before. But her pulled-together eyebrows and her tight mouth, along with how she moved people out of her way with her sheer presence, made her less bohemian and even more angry witch today. I wondered what was going on.

There was nothing I could do to find out, unless I left my stall unattended and went to ask her. Not a good plan with the continual flow of shoppers stopping and passing by.

In between customers, I noticed my phone vibrating in my pocket. I'd been looking at it all morning, until I'd gotten to the market. Since then, it appeared that I'd missed calls from Sam, Allison, and Ian. The current call coming in was from Allison.

"Hey," I said as I answered.

"Did you get my message?"

"No, sorry."

"S'okay. A terrible thing happened this morning."

"I know. A dead body at the bank."

"You know who it was?"

"No."

"It was Robert Ship, one of the men who were at the market yesterday."

I paused. "I thought he was the business office guy."

"He was. No one knows why he was at the bank."

"Oh no. What happened to him?"

"He was killed, Becca."

"Oh no," I repeated. "Did they catch the killer?"

"No, but . . ."

"Just tell me, please."

"Sam took some people in for questioning and he's looking for one other person."

"Who did he take in?"

"Oh, Becca. Peyton, for one. Jeff was also picked up. They had appointments though I'm not clear who with—the bank or Mr. Ship at the bank. It's confusing right now. Lyle Manner, the guy from the bank, was also taken in. But they're also looking for Betsy."

"Betsy?" I said, my thoughts of despair over Peyton pushed to the side for a moment.

I pulled my front table back and stepped around it, merging behind a small group. "Allison, I saw her here, not long ago. She was hurrying down the aisle, I thought she was going to her stall. I'm going there now."

"She was here? At Bailey's?"

"I'm sure I saw her. I'm on my way to her stall to check."

"I'll meet you there."

It didn't take long to get to Betsy's stall even though it felt like it did. As I passed Ian's, I noticed he was with a customer, but he didn't see me pass by. My feet were not able to move as quickly as I would have liked because of the people in my way. It seemed like my destination kept moving farther down the aisle. I arrived at the exact moment Allison arrived. She was breathing heavily enough to make me think she'd run from wherever she'd been.

We looked at each other and then in tandem looked down at the note Betsy had placed on her front table. She'd secured it with a rock but its bottom corners flapped with the breeze stirred up by passing shoppers.

The note said: *Sorry for the short notice, but I will be leaving Bailey's at this time. I hope to make other arrangements to sell my tomatoes soon. Here's my e-mail if you'd like to stay in touch.*

The stall was otherwise empty. No sign of the previous day's bins, or chairs, or cash box. No tomatoes anywhere. Most important, no Betsy.

"She didn't say anything to you?" I asked.

"No, not a word. When I came by her stall earlier, her stuff was here. Well, her tomatoes weren't but her tables were. I thought she just hadn't made it in yet. I told Sam as much when he called looking for her," Allison said.

"She left her e-mail address. Maybe she's not trying to hide," I said.

"Then why didn't she talk to me first?" Allison said. "She and I have never had one moment of difficulty. She could have talked to me about anything."

A thought occurred to me. "Come with me a sec."

Allison followed me back to Ian's stall. He was still with a customer but he saw us peering in this time and waved, making me think it was okay to wait. He joined us a few seconds later.

"Did you try to call me?" I said.

"I did. Well, I meant to call Allison but you two are next to each other in my phone. Then a customer showed up and I didn't have time to fix the mistake. Well, no matter. It's good you're both here. I saw Betsy packing up her stall. She seemed very upset. I tried to talk to her, but she literally waved me away. Wouldn't look at me. Wouldn't say anything. I thought you should know. Sorry I got the number wrong."

"Was she alone?" Allison asked.

"Yes. I really did try to help her get her bins through the back, but she didn't want my help and she managed it pretty quickly."

"Didn't say anything about what was bothering her?"

"No."

"Thanks, Ian. I appreciate it," Allison said.

"She definitely cleared out," I said.

Allison nodded. "Something's up. I'll find her and talk to her. I'm sure we can work out whatever needs to be worked out."

Ian was pulled away by a young man interested in "the biggest yard art" that could be sculpted. Allison gave me a serious look that I read to mean "Follow me." So I did.

A few moments later we were in her air-conditioned office. If I'd been the market manager instead of Allison, I probably would have just sat inside the office all summer and hoped the market vendors didn't need me for anything.

She plopped into her chair and I sat in the one across the desk. The space was small, but more cozy than cramped.

I'd rarely seen my sister flustered. Maybe not ever. She'd always been the reasonable twin, the one who could handle anything, come up with the proper solution to any challenge. Today, though, she looked harried. Her normally smooth, dark ponytail was framed by a few escaped flyaways.

"I will look for Betsy and try to figure out the problem there—well, I suppose if the police don't find her first. Right now, we need to talk about Peyton."

I nodded eagerly. "Allison, I haven't had a chance to tell you something and at this moment it seems like I was avoiding it but I wasn't. I just . . . well, I need to tell you some things about Peyton and another visitor we have in town."

Allison blinked, smoothed her hair, and then listened patiently as I told her about Harry and what he'd shared with me regarding his suspicions of Peyton, and how he'd come all the way across the country just to investigate the Arizona crimes.

"Oh my, Becca. That's all so terrible. Does Harry really think Peyton assaulted someone, or is a thief? I'm not as concerned about stealing the secret recipe, but the assault and the money? That's bad."

I swallowed hard because the next words I had to say didn't want to come out. In fact, I felt like I wanted to cry even as I thought them.

"And now maybe murder?" I finally said.

"Oh, Becca, Mom and Dad are going to freak." Allison deflated.

Though that was probably true, it was an odd first thought to have. I chalked it up to stress, and I nodded in agreement.

Seven

"Harry?" I said as I stepped toward my stall. He was behind the front table, helping my customers.

"Becca. It just seemed like the thing to do," he said as he handed a jar of blueberry preserves and a couple dollars' change to a young man with the best dreadlocks I'd ever seen. "People were wondering where you were. I thought . . . well, it just seemed like it needed to be done."

"Thank you." I smiled as I stepped back behind the table and joined him.

Harry took off his ever-present cowboy hat and pulled a handkerchief out of his pocket. He wiped from his forehead all the way to the back of his neck. "Goodness, the humidity is thick here."

I laughed. "A little different from Arizona. But really,

thanks. I up and abandoned my post. I thought I would come back to an empty stall, and that the customers would have had every right to just take whatever they wanted. If I have to step away, I usually leave a note. You saved my cash flow for the day, and my reputation. Much appreciated."

"My pleasure." He plopped the hat back onto his head.

"I'm glad you're here," I said. Allison and I had agreed that it would do no good to keep the fact that the police wanted to talk to Peyton about a murder from Harry. He and Sam had already met and hit it off if I wasn't mistaken. Sam would surely give Harry the details when they spoke again anyway, not to mention that the news would spread quickly no matter how much we might not want it to. "I need to tell you something."

In between and around two more transactions, I told Harry who had been found dead at the bank and how it seemed that murder was suspected.

He reminded me of Sam momentarily, as his chocolate eyes became extra serious and pensive at the same time. They didn't change colors, though, so not quite Sam's. However, even with their singular shade, they managed to say a lot.

"I will be honest with you, Becca, I would never suspect your cousin could commit murder. She struck me as someone a little . . . I don't know, less than reliable, perhaps desperate, young and not as smart yet as she might be someday, but not a killer. And if she's been in Arizona for a while, how would she have known the victim beforehand? Didn't you mention that she didn't ever live here in Monson?"

"Never. Just visited family. She grew up in Virginia. She just met Mr. Ship yesterday, I'm pretty sure about that. He was going to help the food truck vendors set up temporary business licenses."

Harry shook his head slowly. "I'd like to talk to Sam if he isn't too busy at the crime scene. Where is his office located?"

I gave Harry the simple directions to Monson's small downtown police station.

"You going to be okay without me?" he said.

"I'm not really sure," I said. "You handled everything like a pro. Thanks, Harry."

"My pleasure."

As expertly as his big body could accomplish, he maneuvered around the front table and walked down the aisle toward the market exit. I watched his high cowboy hat move above most of the summer shoppers, some of them in straw hats, but their hats seemed much less important than Harry's.

As with the day before, it didn't take long to sell out of product. I was still ahead with inventory, but I wouldn't be for long if this pace kept up.

I hadn't really expected to come back to an empty stall, because that wasn't the way farmers' market shoppers behaved—no one just took something they wanted. But I had expected a note or two of complaint, or maybe some cash on the table with a note explaining what had been purchased in my absence. As it was, Harry truly had saved the day.

Recently, I'd thought about hiring an assistant. Between the market, the farm, and my continually increasing retail business at the Maytabee's shops, I always had something that needed to be done and I always felt a little behind schedule. Even when I was technically on schedule, a growing to-do list always loomed ahead. The things that had been holding me back from making the hire were tied to my personality. I'd want an assistant to be able to help everywhere and also be completely flexible, at all times. That wasn't fair. I had to fix myself and my inconsistent routine before I brought someone in who'd have to put up with me.

I threw the empty boxes into the back of my truck and closed my stall when it seemed we'd hit a lull in business. I stepped around to the front of Linda's stall just as she was selling what looked like her last pie of the day.

"Hey," she said as she smoothed back her hair. "I hope the big guy who can't possibly be from around here was supposed to be in your stall earlier. I didn't have a chance to talk to him, but he looked like he was doing everything as it was supposed to be done. I couldn't have offered much help at the time anyway."

"He's a friend from Arizona. A police officer," I said.

"Really? What's he doing here?"

"Chasing someone."

"Oh, that's interesting. Tell me more."

I hadn't talked much to anyone other than Sam about what happened in Arizona. The time that had passed mellowed the memories and I found that I enjoyed sharing some of the details with Linda. It was still a scary story, just not as scary as it had been.

And even though a family member and other market vendors were involved in the investigation of Robert Ship's murder, I told Linda everything I knew. She listened intently.

"Becca, your cousin didn't kill anyone," she said when I was done. "I only met her in passing yesterday, but she's not a murderer. It just wouldn't be in her. I have a hard time thinking she could have hurt that restaurant manager, too. Now, stealing a recipe—I don't know. That certainly sounds like something a young, inexperienced person might be tempted to do. It's somehow a less harmful crime in some people's eyes. I hope she didn't, but perhaps if she did, she should let the authorities know as soon as possible. If she did steal it, I bet she's scared to death. At the moment I feel sorry for her. Now, if she proves to be guilty of either assault or murder, I'll take back that sympathy."

Though we were friends, Linda would never say something she didn't mean. I appreciated her comments and insight. I was sure my cousin was scared, but I didn't know how to ease her fears.

"Betsy couldn't kill anyone, either," Linda continued. "Although I wonder about her sometimes. She's a mystery, isn't she?"

"She is. I don't know anything about her family. I suppose we've never been close, but I know a little about almost all the vendors' families."

"I'm in the same boat. I've had some friendly conversations with her, but I don't know one thing about her personal life. I don't even know if she has a significant other. She never brings anyone to the market's family events. She and I live very close to each other, but we've never socialized together. My fault as much as hers, I suppose, but you just get those vibes from some people, definitely from Betsy—'work relationships only.' Now, Jeff—I wouldn't be surprised by anything he did. He's different, and makes me uncomfortable."

"Do you know anything about his personal life?"

"I know he dates lots and lots of women. And doesn't call them the next day if you know what I mean. I wish I didn't know that much, but when he first started working here, I happened to overhear some conversations."

"Yeah, I'm not surprised, either. I wonder how much Allison knows about either of them."

"If anyone knows anything, it would be Allison."

We talked a few minutes more about how Linda's husband, Drew, a Navy SEAL, and Sam seemed to get along so well and how we both thought they were probably plotting ways to save the world whenever they were together. We laughed, but there was a serious ring to the laughter.

I helped her gather her empty boxes and load them in the van. As I waved a good-bye to her taillights, I decided I still had a few things to do before I left for the day.

I hurried toward Jeff's cart; this was much more easily accomplished without the earlier crowd to slow me down. I wasn't surprised to find that it didn't look to have been opened for business today. His table was folded and leaning against the side of the cart. I inspected everything for another note or something that might be important, but I didn't find anything. However, if he'd left the market as permanently as it seemed Betsy had, he would have taken the cart and table with him. Unless he had been picked up by the police before even making it in.

I turned away from the cart and walked back out to the

parking lot. I had a hunch that's where I'd find Allison. But this time the hunch was wrong. There was no sign of her, but someone else captured my attention.

All of the trucks except Peyton's were open for business, their serving counter doors either pushed up or pushed out and supported by sturdy metal rods. Either the trucks' food hadn't quite caught on yet, or business had hit a lull. There were no customers outside any of them. However, the cupcake lady, Basha Bonahan, stood outside Peyton's closed truck, her hands on her hips and her focus on something on the top right part of the side panel.

I made a beeline to her. "Hi," I said.

She started slightly. "Oh! I didn't see or hear you, young lady. Maybe clear your throat or something next time."

"Sorry."

"It's all right." Basha shook her head. "I'm a little jumpy, I guess. Did you hear about the murder?"

"I did," I said

"That man was just here yesterday. He seemed . . . well, I'm not sure he seemed like much of anything, but he didn't seem like someone who would be murdered. Whatever that means, I guess." Tears filled her eyes, but they didn't fall.

"I'm sorry, Basha. This is a terrible shock."

"Oh, I'm fine. Gracious, I didn't even know him. It's just . . . unsettling, that's all. I'm sorry for his family, and I keep looking over my own shoulder."

I nodded.

"Did you know him?" she asked.

"No, not really."

She turned her eyes back to the truck. I inspected her profile as she seemed to recover.

"What are you looking at?" I asked.

Basha blinked and then looked at me again. "Just at the truck. I heard the young woman who owns this one was . . . what's the word? Detained by the police regarding the murder."

I nodded. "I don't really know what's going on, but I thought you were looking at the top corner up there specifically. Is there something about the way the trucks work that made you look there?"

"No, nothing. That's just where my eyes fell," she said.

I didn't quite believe her, but I didn't know why. It was just a side panel—there were no dents, nothing strange.

"Anyway, I guess I should get back. It's been quiet for an hour, but we had business earlier. I hope it picks up some tomorrow." Basha turned and walked quickly away.

The entire exchange left me feeling somewhat confused. She'd been emotional one second, almost taciturn the next. Blatantly curious about the corner of the truck from what I'd observed, and then claiming to me she wasn't looking at anything specific. And then she'd marched back to the duties at hand.

"Hey," I said as I hurried to catch up to her. "I've wanted to be a customer since the second I saw you pull into the lot. I'd love a cupcake."

Basha laughed. "Come on over, I'll hook you up."

Again, her personality shifted. Now she seemed downright jovial. I waited outside as she hoisted herself into the business part of the truck and came over to the counter.

She pointed at the handwritten menu board folded open on the counter, which listed the flavors she'd made today. "What can I get you?"

Key Lime Disco, Maple Bacon Sizzle, Piña Colada Party, Strawberry Cheesecake Swirl, Chocolate Coma, and Lemon Pucker.

"I'll take two of each," I said.

"Dessert for the family?"

"Maybe," I said with a smile.

Basha nodded knowingly.

Shortly, I had the box of cupcakes, but no answers to my questions about what Basha had been looking at. Another customer appeared so I stepped out of the way after our brief transaction, and resumed my search for Allison.

It was by chance (though sometimes I called these incidents twin-moments) that I happened to see her standing at the market entrance by her office building just as she looked my direction and waved me over.

As I passed each food truck, I glanced inside them, ready to wave if the proprietors were available. The only person I was able to greet was Daryl, who stood at the counter of his wing truck and watched me though those tilted glasses. Would it be rude to ask if one of his ears was that much higher than the other or if he'd just done something to bend the glasses? He scowled when he waved and made me uncomfortable. I didn't see either Mel or Hank in their trucks and I wondered where they'd gone, so I stepped up the pace as I hurried toward Allison.

"Cupcakes?" she said with an enthusiastic but weary smile when she saw the box under my arm.

"Couldn't resist," I said.

"I tried one earlier and thought it was delicious. I also had a taco. I recommend Paco, I mean Mel, and his tacos."

"You look tired."

"I am. Peyton's on her way back. Sam's bringing her," Allison said.

"That's good news, isn't it?" I said.

"Peyton's not being held but she isn't in the clear yet. I don't know exactly what that means and I hope you try to get some details from Sam when you can. I told Sam I would be responsible for her. I'll watch her."

"I'll get whatever I can from him. Any word from Jeff?"

"Nothing. I tried to call him earlier, but only a couple of times. Haven't heard from him. Hopefully Sam can give you more information about that, too. Maybe they talked to him today. There they are." Allison nodded toward the parking lot entrance.

A police cruiser moved slowly through the parking lot. It was followed by a smaller car—Harry's rental.

Peyton was seated in the front passenger seat of the cruiser. She glanced at us through the window, making it clear that she was not a happy cousin.

Sam got out of the car first. He opened the door for Peyton at the same time Harry got out of his rental. We became an awkward group of five.

"Allison, Becca," Peyton said as she barely looked up from the ground.

For a long moment the rest of us blinked at each other.

"Peyton needs to stay in town," Sam finally said. "I let

her know that Harry's here because of some trouble in Arizona. She recognized him."

"I haven't done anything wrong," she mumbled as she crossed her arms in front of herself.

"Truthfully, there's not a lot that tells us you *did* do something wrong, Peyton," Sam said. He turned to Allison. "But there are some questions that we need answered before we know for sure. She would like to go ahead and open her food truck tomorrow if it's okay with you."

"Of course. And you'll stay with me, too, Peyton. Okay?" Allison said.

"Or me," I said.

"That won't work," Allison said. "Conflict of interest or something considering you and Sam are dating."

"This is the guy?" Peyton said, uncrossing her arms and standing straighter.

I nodded quickly. Now was not the moment to discuss my love life.

"Well, he hasn't been a complete jerk, I guess," Peyton said.

"That's good," I said evenly.

"Anyway," Sam continued. "It's fine if you want to stay with Allison. In fact, it's what we would prefer."

"Gee, thanks for the permission." Peyton blanched. "Sorry. I'm not happy with how the day has gone and I should be more respectful. Thank you."

She sounded like she meant it. Sort of.

"All right. It's settled. Come with me," Allison said as she gently took Peyton's arm. "Tomorrow's another day. Let me finish a few things in my office and then we can go home."

"Harry, where are you staying?" Sam asked as Allison and Peyton disappeared into Allison's office.

"Small hotel on the way to a town called Smithfield."

"Why don't you stay at my house?" Sam said. "I'm at Becca's most of the time. You'll pretty much have the place to yourself."

Harry seemed momentarily confused by the offer, and then said, "I don't want to impose."

"No imposition," Sam said. "It probably seems empty most days and a potential target for theft. You'll make it look a little lived-in."

Target for theft. I loved it when he talked cop.

"In that case, thanks."

"Get your stuff, and then both of you come over for dinner," I said. "I need to get home to Hobbit."

Arrangements were made, and as much as I wanted Sam and Harry to give me all the details about everything that had happened that day, I knew they wouldn't as we stood in the parking lot. My only hope was that I could get them to talk during dinner. Sam didn't really drink, but I was so curious about the day's events that the idea of liquoring them up crossed my mind.

When I was the only one left outside Allison's office building, I turned to go back through the market and to my stall. But then I stopped as intuition tickled at the back of my neck. I turned around one more time to look toward the trucks. Basha was outside again and looking at the top right corner of Peyton's side panel.

"What in the world?" I muttered.

I had an urge to go back and ask her again, but I knew it wouldn't do any good. I'd have to find a better way to get her to talk to me. I could try to ply her with some strawberry jam. Maybe she could use some for her cheesecake cupcakes.

As I walked past Allison's office, I leaned in to see if I could hear anything, but no sound made it out.

Once in the comfort of my own truck, I set the box of cupcakes on the passenger side of the bench seat and was glad to finally head back home to Hobbit.

Eight

Hobbit was as happy to see me as I was to see her. I kept the distractions at bay during our evening frolic. By the time we'd run around the strawberries and pumpkins a few times, we were both panting. Hobbit found relief in her newly filled water bowl, and I found relief with the tallest glass of iced tea I could pour.

Dinner was grilled burgers and a mix of other stuff I found in the fridge. Tomato and mozzarella salad, with sides of cucumbers and strawberries, went well with the giant burgers.

It was a meal even a big guy like Harry could enjoy. Though he was plenty used to heat, our humidity could take down even the strongest man if he wasn't used to it. The shaded patio was surprisingly comfortable by dinnertime, the heat and humidity both now tolerable. Sam and I told

Harry that we could go into the air-conditioned inside whenever he wanted to. He didn't seem to want to.

"This is beautiful," Harry said after dinner and as he looked back over the rolling hills and toward my crops, which spread up a slope to the side of the house and patio. "So green."

"Though there isn't as much green in the desert, I was surprised to find as much color as I did," I said.

"It's a beautiful place, too. They both are, but in different ways. Arizona is home. I've been out of the state a time or two, but I'm always a little jostled when there isn't any cactus around," Harry said with a smile. He'd removed the hat but he still seemed a little too big for the space he took up—in a good way, though, as if his mere presence invited you into his life. His bigness somehow made you think that if there was room for him, there was also plenty room for you and anyone else. I knew differently, though. In fact, he was more guarded than welcoming, but I was sure his demeanor was a helpful trait for his career choice.

Hobbit shifted on the ground beside my feet. "Any chance I could ask you two some questions? About today?" I said.

"Of course," Harry said.

I'd seen the quick sideways glance Sam and Harry shared when I'd asked.

"We'll answer what we can, Becca. Some of your questions might be either unanswerable at this time or perhaps something we have to keep to ourselves," Sam said.

Again, I loved cop mode.

"Did you tell Sam about everything from Arizona, the things you think Peyton might have been involved in?" I said to Harry.

"Every bit of it," Harry said.

"Sam, what do the Arizona events have to do with your murder investigation? I guess what I'm asking is, is there any reason you can see how everything would somehow be tied together?"

"No way at all," Sam said. "But again, Becca, we can't rule out anything at this point. We don't have enough to disregard any possible connection, however unlikely it may be."

I nodded. "Did Peyton admit to anything yet? Maybe even something she did in Arizona?"

"No," Sam and Harry said.

"Okay," I continued. "What about Betsy? Did you ever talk to her? Did you know she left the market?"

"I did know she left. Allison called me," Sam said. "We haven't talked to Betsy, but . . . well, we think she had an alibi that we've confirmed via a third party. She drove up to the Smithfield market early this morning and talked to the manager there. It was thanks to Allison that we even talked to Smithfield. She didn't think Betsy would want to give up a market business and she thought Betsy might try Smithfield. That's exactly what she did, before she left the note at Bailey's."

"Really? Why would she want to leave Bailey's for Smithfield? I mean, it's a great market, but I don't understand."

"I think Allison would like to have that answer, too. And we still want to talk to Betsy, but she isn't a priority at this point."

Sam looked pointedly at Harry and seemed to contemplate his next words, but I didn't think it was because he was concerned about saying something he shouldn't in front of the other police officer. He just liked to think before he spoke. I needed more of that in me.

"Becca, I'll tell you our theory of the order of events from this morning, if you'd like to know them. You might better understand why we're talking to who we're talking to," Sam said.

I scooted my plate back on the table and leaned on my elbows. I wanted to give Sam my full and undivided attention. I couldn't believe he was offering to share the information, but I tried to hide my surprise and just look matter-of-fact. "Please."

"Right." He'd scooted his chair back from the table. He leaned forward and put his elbows on his knees. "We got the call early this morning, but you knew that part. The call came from Mr. Lyle Manner, an employee at the bank. He found Mr. Robert Ship's body in the parking lot behind the bank."

I interrupted, but I couldn't help myself. "Sam, the whole bankers' hours joke is kind of based in fact. I've never known bankers to get to work early. I'm sure it was just plain weird that Mr. Ship was at the bank in the first place, but what was Mr. Manner doing there so early?"

"Good question, Becca," Harry said.

"Very good." Sam smiled, but only a little. "Yes, they were both there, and both starting their workdays early. Mr. Manner was there to meet your cousin, Peyton." Sam paused and studied me a moment, but then continued. "We're trying to understand the details better, but she claims not to have had a bank account set up in Arizona. It's strange because that's practically impossible to do these days, but we're looking into it, and though the crimes here and the crimes in Arizona aren't necessarily tied together, that bit of news did interest Harry."

"Right," I said to Harry. "You mentioned that there was no way to figure out where Peyton got the money for her truck, that it didn't show up on paper until it appeared in the truck seller's account."

"That's right. Peyton has a personal account, but I never found a business account. To repeat what Sam said, that's a pretty hard thing to do these days, have a business without a business account."

"Nevertheless," Sam continued, "Lyle Manner agreed to meet Peyton early to discuss setting up an account. She requested the early time, and he agreed. She was waiting for him, sitting on the curb on one side of the bank's back parking lot. It wasn't until they were at the back door together—Manner and Peyton—that Manner saw Ship's body off to the left behind a Dumpster. We're not sure why Mr. Ship was at the bank. We hope to find out."

"Oh, no," I said.

"Right," Sam said.

"Peyton was there alone with the body for a while?"

"It appears that way at this time."

"How was he killed?"

"Blunt object, we think an industrial pipe of some sort, to the head, but we don't have the object. The area was searched thoroughly."

"All right." I sat back in the chair, and tried not to look deflated. "So wrong place, wrong time for Peyton, right?"

"That's a possibility . . . ," Sam said. He looked at Harry, who pinched his lips into an even tighter line.

"What?" I said.

"Manner overheard an argument between Peyton and

Ship the day before in the Bailey's parking lot. Peyton was upset and had some harsh works for Mr. Ship."

"I witnessed what might be considered an argument between Peyton and *Mr. Manner*, but I didn't see the one with Mr. Ship," I said. "And was it harsh enough to sound like she was threatening murder?"

"Possibly. But you need to know that Peyton denies saying anything threatening to anyone. She told us that she was just trying to explain to Mr. Ship that she didn't think that the food trucks needed temporary licenses, that when she set up her business in Arizona, she educated herself on the business laws. In fact, she went on to tell me that she even thought of moving her truck to Nevada because sales tax laws are different and beneficial to business owners there."

I nodded. Would it be like Peyton to educate herself on pertinent laws? I had no idea. I knew the young, free-spirited, searching-for-herself Peyton, not the slightly older business-owner Peyton.

"I heard that Betsy and Mr. Ship also argued. I don't want to try to make Betsy look guilty even with an alibi, but it makes me wonder if Mr. Ship was just the argumentative type. Or is there any chance Mr. Manner is mistaking the women in the arguments? Even though they look nothing at all alike."

"It's a possibility, Becca. We're looking more deeply at some of the things your questions bring up."

"Dang, I wish I knew what Betsy and Mr. Ship argued about."

"Us, too."

"Seems so . . . out of proportion, I guess. Why would Betsy leave Bailey's and in such a dramatic way? What about Jeff, the potato cart vendor? You were looking for him, right? I think that's what Allison told me."

"We were looking for him, but that was only because Mr. Manner told us we might want to talk to him. We weren't given any more information than that. We don't know why Manner sent us that direction. We have not spoken with him yet, though we tried to stop by his house, too."

"Has he left town?"

"We're not jumping to any conclusions regarding Jeff. There is no evidence at all that he had anything to do with the murder."

"Again, I don't want to point a finger at someone when it comes to murder, but you should probably know what Jeff and I discussed the day before Mr. Ship was killed."

"I'm listening."

"Me, too," Harry said.

I told them the details of the conversation between Jeff and me. Sam tried not to roll his eyes regarding Jeff's insistence that he didn't need a business license, and he muttered something about how easy it would have been for Mr. Ship just to come talk to the police and they would have been happy to talk to Jeff about his incorrect interpretation of the local licensing laws. Sam took a couple notes and then excused himself inside to make a call. Harry and Hobbit went for a quick walk around my crops and I was left alone with my thoughts. My musings didn't clear up any of the questions by the time we were all gathered on the porch again.

We spent the rest of the evening talking mostly about things that had nothing to do with criminal behavior or police duty. We talked about farming and canning and families. The friendship I'd seen growing between Sam and Harry flourished as we talked and laughed. Again, I was glad Harry was in town and that Sam had the chance to know him, even if I was sorry for the reason.

Fleetingly, and throughout the evening, the memory of Basha looking at Peyton's truck flashed through my mind, but I didn't bring it up. I thought I might tell Sam about it after Harry left, but by the time the evening was over and I'd prepared my inventory for the next day, Sam, Hobbit, and I were too tired to do anything except fall fast asleep.

Nine

I hadn't planned on the next morning's diversion. I was surprised by it, in fact. As I steered my truck toward Monson and Bailey's, I felt a pull that made me turn left at an intersection where I would normally turn right. I just couldn't fight it.

Some of the city's government offices, including the police station where Sam worked, were located in an old, small, but stately brick building in the heart of downtown. But there was another office building across the street from the police station. It was a gray stone structure with two unassuming stories and three carved eagles perched atop its front facade. My parents had shown the eagles to Allison and me when we were little girls, and I hardly ever passed the building without looking up and remembering how my sister and I had been mesmerized by the sculptures.

I parked the truck in front of the gray building and looked in the rearview mirror at Sam's building. He was probably somewhere inside and would know what I was up to the second he saw my truck. But I had a pretty good story ready in case he came over and inquired.

Mr. Ship's business licensing office was in the gray building, but so was the driver's license office. It just so happened that my driver's license was set to expire next month. Normally I wouldn't do anything about that until the month of expiration, but it never hurt to take care of something ahead of schedule every once in a while.

Still glancing back over my shoulder toward the brick building, but not seeing any officer moving in or out of it, I jogged up the front steps of the gray building and went through the front doors.

It was already steaming hot outside, and the cool burst of air that greeted me made me think I could find a way to adjust to an inside desk job. The comfort turned into a shiver of horror as I gave it another moment's thought, so I figured I still wasn't ready to sell the farm.

The driver's license office was through the first door on my left. I hesitated there briefly, but then moved down two more doors to the licensing division. I'd been there a few times myself, usually a day or so before my license expired. Mr. Ship might have helped me, but I didn't remember him specifically, and there'd always been a few people working inside.

The door to the office was all glass. I stood close to it and peered in. Behind the wide front counter, I saw two people, a man and a woman, both probably in their early to mid-twenties. They each sat behind a desk and were facing each other, but not looking at each other. The woman's attention was on a piece of paper she held, and the man's was on his computer screen. There was a door on the back wall that seemed to lead to another office, but the rest of the visible space was filled with worktables and too many file cabinets to count easily.

As I pulled the door open, the two people looked up at me and then at each other and then back at me. I noticed that the woman's eyes were puffy and rimmed in red as if she'd been crying, and the man's face was tight with concern.

"Hi, can we help you?" he said as he stood, signaling to the girl that he would handle this customer. She seemed relieved.

"Sure. Thanks," I said as I approached the counter. I could have just asked about the specifics of regulation 458-098, but it might be too abrupt and strange and misplaced, particularly if I wanted these two to take a quick liking to me so they'd willingly share answers to some of my other questions.

"What can I do for you?" he said. He had a name tag pinned above his heart. It said, "Kyle."

"Hi, Kyle," I said. "First of all, I heard about your co-worker and I'm sorry for your loss."

Kyle's eyebrows came together as if his first instinct was to be suspicious of me, but he recovered quickly and said, "Thanks. It's been quite the shock."

"I'm sure. My name is Becca Robins and I work at Bailey's Farmers' Market . . ."

"I thought you looked familiar," the woman said as she stood and joined us at the counter. "I get jam from you all the time. It's delicious."

"Oh, of course, I recognize you. You normally wear a

perfectly floppy straw hat when you're shopping at the market. Thanks for your support of my jams and jellies." Her name tag said, "Meg."

"You're welcome, and yes, I'm the straw hat girl." She smiled, though it didn't reach her puffy eyes.

I paused. "The reason I'm here is kind of weird and tied to Mr. Ship's visit to the market two days ago. He was there because he was helping some visiting food truck chefs get their temporary business licenses in order, but while there he mentioned that a couple of the market's regular vendors were delinquent on business licenses."

"He told us that when he came back in later that day," Meg said. She cleared her throat. "He mentioned that a couple people would be in yesterday morning to talk to him but I don't know who exactly. Maybe he meant today, though. Are you one of the ones that were delinquent?"

"No," I said. "But has anyone else from the market been in, either yesterday or today?"

"No," Kyle said. "Meg and I opened the office both yesterday and today like we always do. No Bailey's folks have been in at all. We heard about Mr. Ship only a half an hour or so into yesterday morning when someone from the police stopped by—an Officer Norton." He shook his head as if he thought he was either rambling or telling me too much, or maybe it was just still hard to believe that their boss had been killed.

I knew Vivienne Norton was thorough, so if Sam had been surprised last night about the regulation issue, then Vivienne hadn't known about it, either.

"One of the delinquent vendors has a food cart at the market. I was the one to approach him to ask about his li-

cense. I was helping out the market manager." I hoped that
was enough to keep them listening. "Jeff, the cart vendor,
mentioned that he didn't need to have a license because of
a certain regulation. He mentioned the number," I pulled a
piece of paper out of my pocket. "Regulation 458-098."

Meg and Kyle immediately knew what I was talking about.
They both said "Oh" in that long, drawn-out way that made me
know they were way too familiar with Jeff and his regulation.

"Jeff, the man who sells baked potatoes?" Meg said.

"Yes, that's him."

"He was a thorn in Mr. Ship's side since the moment he
set up the cart. Mr. Ship was this close to filing a legal complaint against him. Well, he was patient for a long time, but
basically Jeff's been breaking the law by not having a business license," Kyle said.

"Really?" I said. "Is there any chance you can show me
the regulation?"

"Sure." Meg moved back to her desk. "Come through
and you can read it on my screen. I'll print it out for you, too."

Kyle lifted a hinged counter panel so I could walk through.
He scooted a chair over to the spot behind Meg. I sat in it as
he stood behind her on her other side.

Meg manipulated her keyboard and mouse, and in only
a few seconds a PDF page filled her screen.

"This is direct from the book of regulations. It's the law.
It's just a short few sentences that could maybe be interpreted to mean that carts don't need business licenses, but
it's a pretty big stretch. There, right there." She put the curser
next to the regulation number.

It said, "458-098—Pursuant to resolution 124B of the

Monson City Code, it is deemed that carts (see definition under section 13B) used to cook, bake, or warm food items meant for sale to the public must be inspected by city and/or county food inspectors on a regular basis. The results of the inspections are used to determine the validity of the food cart's business standing."

That was it.

"So Jeff was saying that that was the *only* means for determining his business's legal and good standing?" Basically, he was just being a jerk, but I didn't say that part out loud.

"Exactly. And he dug his heels in big time," Meg said.

"Why didn't Mr. Ship file a legal complaint sooner? I mean, other regulations surely must overrule this regulation, right?"

"Right," Meg said.

"It's Monson and we're nice people," Kyle chimed in. "Mr. Ship was great with the business office here, Becca, but he was also willing to help people out if they needed it." I'd turned my head toward Kyle as he spoke, so I didn't miss the looks that he and Meg gave each other, as if to say they knew that Mr. Ship had been way too accommodating with far too many people. The only thing missing from their shared glance was an eye roll. But Kyle continued, "At first he wondered if Jeff might have a point, but when he researched it, he realized that even carts need business licenses. It was all ridiculous, and I thought Jeff was just trying to get away with something as a matter of ego."

Or he was just being a jerk, but again I didn't say it out loud.

"Got it," I said.

I really didn't get it, though. Why wouldn't Jeff just get

a license? They weren't expensive. Was it merely the "jerk" factor? Why pick that to be a jerk about?

"When I first got my business license, I had to answer a bunch of questions regarding whether or not I'd been in any legal trouble and if so what the nature of it had been. I haven't had to answer those questions when I've simply renewed, so I don't remember what they were," I said.

"Here's the application." Kyle stepped around us and moved to the front counter again. He pulled a piece of paper off a stack and returned it to me.

It was the uniform business license application. The questions were pretty basic and close to what I remembered regarding the applicant's past possible legal issues. Things like, have you ever been convicted of a felony? Have you ever been sued? Have you ever been in arrears on child support payments?

Perhaps Jeff had some legal problems he didn't want to come to light?

Or he was just being a jerk.

"Can I ask you about another business?" I said.

"Business licenses are public information," Kyle said. "But I suppose the only information we have is if the license is current or not."

"Betsy's Tomatoes. I think that's what she calls it."

Meg maneuvered the keyboard and mouse again. "Right here. Yes, it . . . oh, nope, the license expired just last month so it's showing past-due, but we give a thirty-day leeway, so it's in a 'pending' file."

"Had it been current before that?"

"Yes, it looks like the original license was issued four and a half years ago with no sign of delinquency," Meg said.

"Why would she be late? And why would she be so upset about it?" I said aloud but to myself.

"Excuse me?" Meg said.

"Who? Betsy?" Kyle said.

"Oh, I'm sorry. I'm thinking aloud," I said.

They shared another look, but I thought this one was because they were trying to figure out what I was up to, what I was really trying to find out with all my questions.

"Can I ask about Mr. Ship's personality? I know it might seem like I'm disrespecting the dead, but that's not it at all. It's just . . . well, I heard that a couple of the market vendors argued with him. The manager isn't happy that they weren't up to date with their licenses, so I'm just trying to see if I can get them off the hook a little. Any chance Mr. Ship would have been being difficult enough to warrant the vendors being touchy?"

They weren't offended, but they weren't quite sure what to say. Their hesitation was obvious.

"I'm sorry," I said, letting *them* off the hook. "That wasn't fair of me to ask."

"It's okay," Kyle said. "But I'm not sure either of us can answer that very well. Mr. Ship was a good boss. That's probably all we should say."

"I understand," I said. I tried to figure out what they *weren't* saying, but there were too many possibilities to speculate. "Do you have any idea why he was at the bank early yesterday morning?"

There was a chance that he was killed elsewhere and his body was taken to the bank, but I didn't think that's what had happened. I'd have to ask Sam if they knew that much yet.

"We have no idea. He and a man who works at the bank were good friends, so we wonder if they were supposed to meet for breakfast or something. But we weren't told about such a meeting. Meg and I have discussed that a few times, wondering if we missed a comment."

The door to the office swung open and we all turned to watch a young woman come through. She was tall and dressed to the nines in a suit and heels. She was unfamiliar to me, but both Meg and Kyle seemed to recognize her.

"I've taken up enough of your day. I hope I haven't interrupted your schedules," I said.

"Not at all," Meg said as she handed me a copy of the PDF page that noted the regulation.

I told them both thank you and Kyle lifted the counter again for me as I walked through.

I made my way toward the glass door and turned back to look at them. Kyle looked up and I mouthed, "Sorry again for your loss."

He nodded a quick thank-you.

As I walked past the driver's license office, I still had some time before I had to be at Bailey's. I could get my license taken care of right now and I wouldn't have to come back in a month. But I noticed something outside that was more interesting. Harry's rental car was parked across the street at the end of a line of three police cruisers. I was curious enough to come back later for the license and go see if I could find Harry instead.

I stepped out into the heat, crossed the street, and climbed the stairs up to the brick building. Inside, it was comfortably cool, but not as frigid as the gray building. I took the short flight of stairs two at a time up to the second floor, walked past a receptionist in the hallway who had seen me enough times that I was of no real interest to her, and through the door marked simply "Police."

Harry was easy to spot. He was standing next to Sam's desk as Sam sat in his chair, his focus on his computer monitor. Neither of them noticed me enter.

"Becca, what's up?" Officer Vivienne Norton said as she stopped in front of me. Officer Norton was a contradiction with her thick makeup, big bleached blond hair, and burly muscular frame that any guy would be proud to have.

"Just stopping by to see Sam but it looks pretty busy around here."

Officer Norton nodded and said, "It is, but go on in. I suppose he can tell you himself if he's too busy to gab."

"Thanks."

It was, indeed, busy. I knew most of the Monson police officers but not all of them. I darted and dodged around a few of them before I made it to Sam's desk. I tried not to be in the way when I visited the station, but it would have been an impossible task today; there were just too many people in the big room.

"Hey, Becca," Sam said quickly and distractedly.

"Becca." Harry smiled and lifted his hat briefly.

"Hi," I said. I looked at Harry. "What's going on?"

"Sam's looking at some of my case files regarding the theft of the deposit money."

"Oh. May I look, too?" I asked.

Sam looked over at Harry.

"I think it'll be all right," Harry said. "There's nothing there we've tried to keep secret."

I stepped around to the spot behind Sam and looked at the screen to see a page filled with a bunch of disconnected numbers. I'd have to lean down and in to read it closely, but I could understand that it must be about money.

"When you followed the money, where did it go?" I said. We'd talked about Peyton's account and the truck seller's account, but I suspected they were looking at the money that disappeared after the assault on the manager.

Dating Sam had given me a front row seat to the world of criminal activity. There were still plenty of people behaving illegally. Bad things happened, but more and more bad guys were getting caught because it was becoming so difficult to get away with anything. Security cameras were helpful, DNA could be examined, a skin cell or two were exactly like leaving your driver's license at the scene of a crime. It was astonishing how many criminals left their phones behind.

And theft, embezzlement. How did anyone accomplish such a thing anymore? Offshore bank accounts? Real money was rarely touched nowadays. Transactions were electronic and made money all but invisible, though no less valuable. Of course, people like me still worked in a world of mostly cash, but I was getting closer and closer to setting up a merchant account so that I could take credit cards simply by plugging a small card reader into my phone. Money was vapor, but still necessary.

"The restaurant manager was taking the money to the bank.

She was accosted by someone who fit the description of your cousin, though the perpetrator was disguised enough to confuse the witness during a lineup. Your cousin couldn't be identified with one hundred percent certainty," Harry said.

"That seems like a good thing for Peyton."

"It's why she's free. But the witness is still pretty sure it was her. Same build, same type of hair. But the thief wore a cap and sunglasses . . . and seemed to have a facial scar."

"Seemed to? Peyton doesn't have a scar."

"It's what the witness saw. It could have been makeup."

"As the manager was walking down the street with a bank bag of money, someone who looked mostly like Peyton but with a scar on their face assaulted the manager and stole the money?" I said, thinking I should throw in something about a one-armed man, but I held back.

"Yes."

"It was a deposit. A large one, right? Fifty thousand dollars?" I said.

"Right. Well, the manager had been out of town for the entire week. Peyton had been in charge, and she didn't take any deposits in during the week. She claims she was told to keep the money in the safe and that the manager would take it in when she got back. The manager denies giving such an instruction." This was a repeat of the information Harry had given me earlier, but I listened extra closely just in case he added something he hadn't told me before. He didn't.

"That's some busy restaurant." I whistled.

"And that was a slow week. It's a very popular place."

Sam turned to Harry again. "Video?"

"Sure. Again, we haven't tried to keep it a secret. We had the local news stations run it."

"Uh-oh, do I want to see it?" I said.

Sam shrugged. "It's inconclusive."

"Okay, roll it."

Sam moved and clicked the mouse, and a black-and-white video appeared on the screen.

"This is the manager. The money bag is insider her bigger bag," Harry said as he pointed at a person dressed in shorts and a T-shirt with a messenger bag slung over her shoulder. She walked down the sidewalk at a confident, quick clip. She looked nothing like Peyton. She was tall with an athletic body. Even with the poor quality of the security camera video, I noticed her muscular legs and arms. A ponytail stuck out of the back of the baseball cap on her head.

Just at the second before she would have stepped out of range of the camera, another person, someone dressed in long sleeves, long pants, and an even bigger baseball cap than the one the manager wore ran up to her and pushed her back a step or two and then down to the ground, hitting her on the arm with a pipe. The attacker dropped the pipe, violently grabbed the messenger bag, and then ran in the other direction out of the range of the camera.

The manager held on to her arm, rolled back and forth a couple times, and then gathered herself. An elderly man passing by helped her up, and seemed to want to make sure she was okay. She doubled over for a second and he pulled out a cell phone. But she stood upright another second later and waved away his cell phone efforts. She grabbed her own phone from her pocket and then hurried out of the picture, leaving the elderly man to rub his chin as he watched her go.

"It was quick," I said. "And the person who took the bag was really only in the picture for a couple seconds and only part of them could be seen."

"Yep, that's why it's inconclusive," Sam said.

"Why would you think that might be Peyton?" I turned to Harry.

"Watch it again. The build of the person, and if you look really closely, you can see some hair sticking out from under the cap. It looks like her short, dark, curly hair."

"But lots of people have short, curly, dark hair," I protested.

"Yes, but look again. Look at the build—very feminine. Very easily could be Peyton."

"All right, play it again, Sam," I said. Harry and Sam both smiled at me.

Sam played the video again, and I looked for the curled hair, and the build of the obviously female attacker. And I saw what they were saying. Sort of. There was certainly enough doubt in my mind that it could be called "reasonable" if the video was the only evidence used to try to convict my cousin. A jury could never determine for certain that that was Peyton, I didn't think.

I was relieved a little, but not enough because Harry was correct—there was a chance that it was Peyton.

"Peyton is not a mean person," I said. "I cannot imagine her knocking someone over with that sort of force, and hitting someone? I can't see her doing such a thing. I can't vouch for the amount of strength someone might need to do that, but Peyton's just . . . not like that." I knew it wasn't enough to deter Harry.

"First of all, though the manager's arm was pretty bruised, it wasn't bad. The hit wasn't hard. The resulting concussion from the fall was minor, but any concussion is bad. It could have been much worse, or it could have been a blow to the head with the pipe, which . . . well, who knows? Besides, I thought you hadn't seen her for some years. People change, Becca, particularly if they are desperate, and people get desperate about money," Harry said.

"Right," I said. "Sam, one more time, please."

As he played the video one more time, I looked at it extra hard. And I still didn't feel strongly one way or another about the identity of the person with the curly hair and the pipe.

It just wasn't enough.

Sam had to switch gears when one of the other officers called him over to another desk. Harry sat in Sam's chair and played the video again. I decided I didn't want to watch it anymore, so I tried to scoot away and out of the office without much fanfare.

However, I didn't get far out of the station when Harry caught me going down the stairs.

"Where're you going, Becca?" he said.

"Bailey's. Why?"

"Sam wondered if you'd want to come with me first."

"Where are you going?" I resisted the urge to check the time on my phone. I was sure I was later than I should be.

"I told Sam I was going to drive out to Betsy Warren's house, just to see if she's there by some chance."

"Really? What would she have to do with Peyton's Arizona issues?"

"Allegedly she had an issue with Mr. Ship. Allegedly so did Peyton. Neither of them is telling the truth about it. I'm trying to understand Peyton better. I won't be official, and you won't, either. We'll just be casual, friendly-like. Sam doesn't think we'd be in any danger. Wanna—?"

"Yes!" I said before he could finish the invitation.

"Good. I think you should drive. If she's there, your truck will be nonthreatening. She might not want to answer the door if she sees some big old Indian with a cowboy hat knocking. Your truck will ease the way." He smiled, crinkling his eyes and causing me to smile back at him. "Again, Sam thinks there's no chance at all that you and I will be in danger, but you still have to promise to let me be in charge if I need to be."

"Deal. Let's go."

Ten

I knew exactly where Betsy lived, even though I'd been there only one time before when she was ill and needed someone to pick up some tomatoes she'd promised a customer. As Linda and I had discussed, they lived close to each other, only a couple blocks apart, but their worlds were very different. Linda and Drew lived in a residential neighborhood that happened to have big backyards. Linda's was perfect for growing a variety of berries and other fruits to use in her pies. Linda and Betsy had infrequently helped each other by getting items to and from the market if one of them couldn't make it. The one time I'd helped Betsy was when Linda had been out of town.

Though Betsy's street was also considered residential, once you turned onto it, you were transported into a world of small farms. The houses were all older miniature versions of "regular" farmhouses. The plots of land weren't all that much smaller than those on Linda's street, but the style of homes along with fewer trees and more crop rows made Betsy's street seem like it was out in the country, not just a turn or two away from town.

I loved my house and my farm, but I'd always loved Betsy's street, too. The houses, most of them with some peeling paint, were homey and welcoming, and the plots of land always seemed just the right size for a one-person farm. Even when I was a little girl and had no idea what my future would be, I enjoyed riding through the neighborhood with my parents and thinking about the types of crops I'd like to grow.

True to form, Betsy's house had some peeling white paint on the clapboard siding. However, it stood sturdy and straight with two stories, tall windows, and a front porch made for rocking chairs and lots of glasses of iced tea. I parked the truck and Harry and I hurried up the three short steps onto the porch. Two green wicker rocking chairs were angled perfectly for the small center table to hold beverages and books at arm's length. A paperback was currently open face-down on the table, and the cushions on both the chairs were worn and indented, making me think they'd been sat in often.

The screen door was closed and locked, but the inner door was wide open and I could see into the dining room. A long walnut table filled the middle of the space and currently held a few boxes. There were some built-in shelves along the back wall where Betsy displayed lots of different patterns of china. The one other time I'd been to her house,

I had wanted to inspect the patterns but hadn't had the time. The wall of shelves was still just as inviting.

I knocked on the screen door. "Betsy! You home?"

Even though I'd tried the handle on the screen door already, I tried it again. Still didn't open.

"Would it be like her to leave her door open if she left?" Harry said.

"Maybe. I used to keep my doors unlocked. Lots of people around here do, but I didn't see her truck. Come on, let's check around back."

Harry followed me as we walked over her small front lawn and then along a side patch that could have used some grooming, but wasn't too unruly.

The barn in the back was more like an oversized garage. It was behind the house, at the end of a gravel driveway that I'd heard Betsy say she wanted to have filled with concrete at some point. The garage was white clapboard like the house, but with lots more peeling paint. It was the shape of a barn, but the one lifted garage door told us that her truck was there, tucked in at just the right angle that no one could see it from the front of the house.

She had about two acres in the back. The acres were filled with lined-up rows of different-sized tomato plants. The growing season in this part of South Carolina was long, and Betsy knew how to stagger her crops so she was able to sell fresh tomatoes throughout the summer and the fall, and still have plenty to make her spaghetti sauce.

The plants looked healthy and well taken care of, but there was no Betsy.

"Her truck's here," I said. "Let's check the back door."

We stepped through another screen door. But this screen was part of an entire set of screens around a back porch. This porch wasn't about paperbacks or iced tea, but where Betsy kept her gardening supplies, including a number of pairs of both boots and gloves—there were muddy sets of each on the floor of the porch. I crouched and touched the mud on the gloves closest to the house door, confirming that it was still wet.

Just as I started to stand again to knock on the door, it swung open, missing my head by a close inch.

"Becca! What in the world?" Betsy said as she stood in the doorway.

"Hi, Betsy," I said. "Harry and I just came out to see how you were doing."

Betsy didn't look happy to see either of us. I was frequently struck by her natural beauty, her peaches and cream complexion. Her clear blue eyes might never have seen a touch of makeup and were lined with the kind of thick brown lashes that made even nonvain women a little jealous. Today, she had her long straight hair held back by a tie-dyed bandanna, and even though her expression was irritated, her face was appealing.

"Who are you?" she said to Harry.

"Oh, I'm sorry," I said. "This is my friend Harry. I met him when I was in Arizona. He's . . . visiting."

Harry took off his cowboy hat. "Nice to meet you."

"You, too," Betsy said abruptly. "Excuse me." She stepped out of the doorway and around me and Harry. She grabbed a woven big-brimmed hat that had been hanging on a hook by the outer door and put it on her head. "I have some work to do. What can I do for the two of you?" She left the screened patio before we could answer.

"Can I just ask her some questions?" I said quietly to Harry.

"Of course. She'll respond better to you than to me."

We followed Betsy out to her tomatoes, about halfway down a row, where she crouched to her knees. She plucked ripe and ready tomatoes off one of the plants and placed them gently into a basket. Even with the big brim of the hat hiding her face, I could see the impatience with each quick pluck. I'd never seen such a thing before. Betsy wasn't always cheery, but mostly she was serene and even-tempered. I was suddenly concerned about her.

"Betsy," I said as we stopped next to her, both Harry and I careful not to step on any of her plants, "what in the world is going on? What happened to make you leave Bailey's? Did we do something wrong? Are you going to the Smithfield market?"

It was miserably hot. I was covered in a thin layer of summer perspiration, and I was sure that Harry was trying to understand and fight the maniacal mix of humidity and heat but he wasn't complaining. Betsy, in her Betsy-way, didn't look bothered by the heat, though she was bothered by something.

"My exit from Bailey's?" she said as she plucked a tomato from the vine so forcefully that the entire plant came out of the ground. She looked at the exposed roots and I thought she might cry.

"Yes, I suppose that's a good place to start," I said.

Betsy separated the tomato from the vine and placed it in the basket. She sighed as she put her gloved hands on her knees. "I'm sorry about that. I will apologize to Allison. I know I handled it extremely poorly, but I had to get out of there. I was angry. I'm also not legally supposed to sell tomatoes in this county at this point, I don't think, and I didn't want Bailey's to get in any trouble because of me."

"I don't understand. What were you angry about?" I thought briefly about telling her about her license's "pending" status, but it wasn't my place and seemed like the least of whatever battles she was fighting.

"It's private, Becca. But it has to do with the man who works at the county license office. I . . . I know him on a personal level and I felt—no, I feel—like he's taking a personal situation that's uncomfortable and attempting to harm my business, or prevent me from doing business."

A bunch of somewhat connected thoughts ran through my mind. I didn't know anything about Betsy's personal life, the romantic parts included. I didn't know Mr. Ship at all. I tried to imagine the two of them together and the picture wouldn't form all the way. Betsy was significantly younger than Mr. Ship had been, but I should know better than to judge relationship age differences.

I also thought she'd missed the bad news.

"Oh," I said. I swallowed hard. "I'm sorry but I wonder if you know the latest development."

She looked up at me, her eyes wide in what seemed like genuine question under the brim of the hat.

I looked at Harry. Not long ago I made a conscious wish that I would never again have to be the messenger of news that included murder. I'd made that wish about the same time I wished that I'd never find a dead body, ever again. But the moment had arrived when it would have been cowardly not to tell Betsy myself. Harry knew that, too. He nodded me on.

"Betsy," I said as I crouched and put my hands over hers. "Mr. Ship is dead. He was killed yesterday morning."

I looked at her closely. I wanted to watch every second of her reaction so that I could tell Sam what I saw. I wasn't an expert, but it sure seemed like the shock and disbelief on her face were not part of an act.

"Becca, are you sure?" she asked.

"I'm afraid so," I said. "I'm sorry if you and he were friends."

She blinked and then her eyes moved to the ground as if she needed something bland to look at for a second. A moment later she looked up at me and said, "We weren't friends. He was my uncle. My father's brother."

It was that moment that I remembered that Betsy's mother had died a few months earlier. She'd gone suddenly from a heart attack, and Betsy had been devastated. That was the first I'd ever heard about her family, and I was embarrassed that I hadn't remembered earlier. I knew nothing about her father.

"You said he was killed," she said. "Do you mean murdered?"

"Yes."

"Oh, no, that's terrible. Really terrible. I need to talk to my dad, Becca. I've been in Smithfield, I've been ignoring the phone, but I bet they've tried to call me. I need to go."

She stood and stepped around both me and Harry as she hurried back to the house. As her legs moved quickly, she shed the gloves and the hat, dropping them on tomato plants. I thought she wasn't even aware of what she was doing.

"That seemed like real surprise. I don't think she killed him," I said.

"Hmm," Harry said noncommittally.

If it had been Sam instead of Harry, he probably would have reminded me that the evidence was the only thing that was important at this point. Harry didn't know me well enough to school me in police procedure.

"Should we just go?" I said.

"Probably," Harry said. He stepped carefully between the rows of tomato plants and then stopped when he reached one of Betsy's gloves. "I think you should accidentally take one of those gloves."

"What?" I said as I looked toward the house.

"I do. I think you should."

"That sounds like theft."

Harry shrugged. "I think you should accidentally take it. You can bring it back at some point. Despite what you might have heard in movies, getting fingerprints from the insides of gloves is a tricky business, but it's possible. Sam might need it. If you happen to have it—by accident—well, it might help."

"But I don't think Betsy's guilty of anything and I think she has an alibi from what Sam said." I was still watching the back of the house.

"Suit yourself." Harry took off again, he and his cowboy hat trudging toward the side of the house. A man I knew, but maybe didn't know at all. Someone from Arizona; a stranger and a friend all in one.

I hesitated but only for a second or two before I picked up a glove and put it in my pocket. I felt terrible and hoped that Betsy hadn't seen what I done.

Truth be told, though, the entire petty larceny thing was also a little thrilling.

Eleven

"Wait, you put pineapple on hot dogs?" I said to Peyton as I held a spatula in one hand and a piece of laminated paper with her hot dog preparation instructions in the other. She'd hastily tied an apron around me and pointed me toward the paper before I could even tell her hello.

I'd been late to the market, but the medium-sized crowd hadn't arrived until late morning/early afternoon anyway. None of my customers seemed to have been looking for me, and I sold out a few hours later, with no complaints regarding my tardiness. The sheer routine of the day had been a welcome respite from the recent interruptions and catastrophes.

It was after I'd closed my stall, about midafternoon, that for some unexplained reason, the trucks' popularity suddenly took off. It was as if the entire county had at once heard about Bailey's temporary culinary treats on wheels, and everyone wanted to come see and sample every single item. A number of the market vendors had been recruited to help with the trucks. I'd volunteered to help Peyton. How hard could hot dogs be?

"Yep, it's really good," Peyton said as she turned a hot dog on the grill. "But my best seller is the Tsunami. It's the one I make with my special sauce."

The recipe you allegedly stole? I thought as I inspected her for any sign of guilt. I saw none.

"Can I help you?" Peyton said to a customer.

The space was tight, so when I took the step to my right to help with the hot dogs she'd already put on the grill, we were directly next to each other. Two people could work in the space, but it would take some time to choreograph the moves well.

I donned some gloves and lifted the end of a hot dog with a fork to inspect its underneath parts. Peyton didn't make just hot dogs on buns. All of her hot dogs were open-faced sandwiches, made with two grilled hot dogs, cut and butterflied, and one thick piece of homemade white bread. The hot dogs had to be grilled to just the right doneness, and she'd mastered it. It might take me a time or two, but I was ready to give it a shot.

"That's going to be a Greek Dog. It's ready," she said when she saw what I was doing. She held out a paper boat with a slice of bread. "Feta cheese, olives. Really good."

I forked up the dogs and placed them on the bread. Peyton added the toppings, explaining the proper amounts to me, and then handed the plate out to a customer whose eyes were big with anticipation.

"Go ahead and get started on a Tsunami. That's what was just ordered. I'll get the next couple orders and then help you at the grill. The Tsunami is really easy. Just the dogs, the bread, the sauce, and some sautéed onions. I always make a bunch of onions, because I use them for a few of the dogs. The Tsunami is not only my best seller, it's also the the easiest one to make."

I looked at the instruction sheet and tried to follow it and watch the dogs on the grill. I was slow, but not too terrible. As I worked on one sandwich, Peyton worked on two or three more. By the time I started my third dog, though, I'd sped up enough to think I might be more of a help than a detriment.

We served a few market vendors, who all cheered me on. Hank, Mel, and Basha also ordered Tsunamis, each of them stopping by when the lines outside their trucks slowed. Both Hank and Mel tried to flirt with Peyton, but it was a waste of their romantic energy. We were too busy for Peyton to notice. In fact, I wondered if Peyton even recognized them as other food truck vendors. She'd been the last one to arrive, and I didn't know if proper introductions had taken place, or if in her eyes they'd just been a couple guys who'd helped set things up. Introductions weren't going to happen with the line of eager hot dog customers continually growing behind them.

By the time the rush of customers dwindled down to something manageable for one person, I decided that Peyton and I could work together just fine if we had to again. We'd nailed the choreography.

"Thanks for your help, Becca. I don't think I could have done that without you. Some people would have walked away," she said.

"My pleasure." I leaned my hip against the outside frame of the grill. "How are you doing, Peyton? You okay?"

She forced a smile and shrugged. "I'm okay. It was really good to get to work today."

"You've been in Arizona for what? A while, I think," I said.

"A couple years now."

"Did you originally go there for a job?" I knew the answer, but I had to start somewhere.

Peyton laughed. "No, I went there for a boy. Bad idea."

"Oh," I said. I was genuinely surprised. I thought she'd just been in search of herself. "It usually is. Didn't work out?"

"Didn't even last a week when I got there."

"I'm sorry."

"No matter. But that meant I needed a job very soon after I got there. I never went to college, Becca. I've worked with food a long time. I hoped for a chance to *really* work with food, perhaps go to culinary school, but things haven't worked out that way. I found a job in a great restaurant down there. I made it into the kitchen and got some real training and some management experience. I know so much more now."

"Why didn't you stay at the restaurant?"

Peyton shrugged and I was struck again by how pretty she was. I wondered if she was tall enough to be a model. She continued, "The truck. I thought it sounded like a cheaper way to have my own restaurant. Now; not down the road after I actually made it to and completed culinary school. That seemed like something that was so far away."

"You glad you got it?"

"Yeah, except that I left the restaurant poorly since they

think I stole their sauce recipe." She nodded at the container of Tsunami sauce sitting beside the grill.

"You mentioned yours was *like* theirs, but not exactly. It's okay to try to copy something using your own tastebuds and experience."

"Yeah, I guess," she said. "This is my recipe, Becca. I never even knew their recipe. The owner of the restaurant was the only one who made it. Top secret. He made it in the middle of the night when no one else was in the place. I couldn't have known the recipe if I wanted to. I made my own. Granted I got the idea because of theirs, but this isn't theirs."

"I get that, but maybe you can understand their position?" I said.

"I worked hard for them. I created a new dish that they're selling very well. I might have liked their sauce enough to create one of my own, but I was good for them, too." She sounded bitter.

"That's good to know," I said. "They were *that* upset about the sauce? Accusatory?"

"Well, there was more, but cross my heart, Becca, I did not do what they think I did."

"What was that?"

"They thought I stole some money." She wouldn't look at me as stress or strain or something pulled at her voice. Even with her head down, I could see the corner of her eyes pinch.

"Oh. That's a terrible thing to be accused of," I said.

Her head popped back up. "I didn't take the money. I didn't hurt anyone. I wouldn't. In fact, I think I was set up."

"Set up?"

"Yeah." Peyton looked at me as if she was struggling with whether I was a good guy or a bad guy. I waited for her to remember she could trust me. "Before the manager left for vacation, she told me to keep all the deposits in the safe, not to take anything to the bank until she got back."

"That seems like a bad idea," I said. *And not something any manager in their right mind would ask of one of their employees.*

"I know. I thought so, too, but when I questioned her about it, she just said that she didn't want me out of the restaurant during the bank's hours, that she needed me in the restaurant more than the money needed to be in the bank, that it would be okay in the restaurant's safe for a week."

I squelched a sarcastic chuckle. There is no way I would have done what Peyton is claiming the manager told her to do. I would have found a way to get the money into the bank account, particularly considering the large amount I knew we were talking about. But, again, my cousin was young, so either she was lying or had been terribly naïve. It could be either one.

"I see," I said. "But I still don't understand how you were set up."

"The day the manager got back into town, she was taking the money to the bank. She got attacked and the money was stolen."

"That's awful. They blamed you for that?"

She nodded. "They think I'm the one who took it. They think I attacked the manager and took the money from her."

"What does she say?"

"She could see the face of the person who attacked her. They had a scar, she thought, but other than that, she thought they looked like me. The police have a video that shows a little of what happened, and even I have to admit the attacker looks a little like me. Kind of. But it wasn't me! I didn't do it."

"Do you have an alibi for the time of the attack?"

"I was on my way in to the restaurant. I walked down that same street a few minutes after the attack. I was on the other side of the street and no video cameras captured my image."

"Not the strongest of alibis."

"No, but that's why I think I was set up. I think the manager took the money herself. I think the police will find it with her if they look hard enough. Think about it. She wasn't hurt badly. She knew there was someone she could pin the crime on, at least divert the police away from thinking it was her. Doesn't that make sense? It's kind of a perfect crime."

She had a point, but it was still a stretch. Ultimately, it was about the money. Was the money that Peyton used to buy her truck the same money that was stolen from the manager? If it wasn't, where did it go? Someday that question would surely be answered. The money trail would ultimately become clear.

I wanted to just come out and ask how she'd paid for the truck, but I had a sense that if I did that at this moment she might shut down. I would get an answer, but not right this second. I needed to build a few more layers of trust first.

"I think the police will figure it out," I said.

"That guy who followed me here to South Carolina is pretty sure I'm guilty. I can tell that much."

Harry was a good friend, no matter how quickly our friendship had been formed. There were valid reasons I liked him so much. Some of them had to do with saving my life.

But Peyton was my cousin. And family was always family and always came first.

Except I just couldn't be sure.

"Probably," I said because there was no point in lying. "He wouldn't have followed you here if he hadn't thought you might be guilty."

"I'm having a lot of 'wrong place at the wrong time' moments. I was at the bank before anyone else yesterday morning so I could get business things taken care of early. How was I supposed to know there would be a dead body by the Dumpster?"

"Unless you put it there, I guess there would be no way for you to have known."

"Exactly."

I thought it was a strange response, but not necessarily suspicious. Her current overriding concern was about her issues in Arizona. Mr. Ship's murder seemed either less important or maybe less real to her. I wasn't sure what that meant, but I hoped it was because murder was so far away from something she could fathom doing.

"Right, well, I'm sure everything will be fine. It will work out, Peyton. But I gotta say, if you can offer Harry, the officer from Arizona, anything that might show your innocence, I suggest you do so. Quickly. Or if you know something about some small part of it, jump in and tell him. Or just tell me. We'll figure something out before we go to the police."

Peyton got busy straightening and cleaning. Most of the motions were unnecessary, but I'd been known to move empty jars from one table to another one just to have something else to focus on for a second or two.

"Dinner at your parents' house tonight?" she said as she brushed some invisible crumbs off the counter.

"I hadn't heard about that."

"Oh. Shoot. I think Allison told me I was supposed to tell you. There was something else, too." Peyton stood straight and bit her bottom lip. "You're supposed to bring something."

"I can call Allison," I said as I pulled out my phone.

"Lavender oil. Does that make sense? Your mom wants to make something with lavender oil. Allison said you could get it from one of the vendors in the market."

Allison had probably told Peyton about the oil early this morning. If she or anyone had mentioned it to me, I could have called Ian and asked him to bring some into the market if he was coming in today. Considering the time, I was now going to have to either find lavender oil someplace else, or go out to his farm. Even when he spent time at Bailey's, he was never here this late.

I'd also been terribly remiss about visiting George, and as time had passed, my embarrassment over that oversight had grown. Maybe it was time to take care of that.

Besides, there was nothing wrong with going out to an old boyfriend's farm to pick up some lavender oil, even if a small sense of discomfort did buzz in my chest for a second.

Which, I realized, was silly and immature.

"Thanks, Peyton," I said. "I'll take care of it."

Twelve

Ian's farm was outside Monson's city limits and just past the small house Allison and I had lived in when we were kids. He'd taken a plot of less than ideal land and turned it into something spectacular. Though I hadn't seen it for some time, I'd heard about the combination house-warehouse that was almost finished and the rows of healthy, purple-flowered lavender plants that rolled idyllically up the short hillside. Allison had described it as a modern-ish storybook setting, a place where you felt like you could grab a book and stretch out on a giant, soft purple comforter for a few hours. As I pulled my truck to a stop on the side of the road, I concurred with her assessment.

The lavender was truly beautiful, something that belonged in a Van Gogh painting, a purple escape on a sunny day. The wide, two-story house had modern lines, but they were mellowed by green clapboard siding and wide white window shutters, creating a charming new twist for the old farmhouse. The house was big, but I knew the living space took up only about half of it. The other half was a work space for Ian's yard art and his multifaceted lavender business. I wasn't sure where George's apartment was located, but I knew it was in there somewhere.

Ian stepped out of the house's side door just as I got out of the truck.

"Becca, hey," he said when he turned to see who'd was attached to the sound of a door shutting. He put down a long metal piece, wiped his hands on his jeans, and walked down a small slope next to the lavender crops. "This is a great surprise. What's up?"

"My mom needs some lavender oil. I didn't get the message until just a little bit ago. Sorry to barge in."

His eyebrows came together as he stopped in front of me. "You're not barging in. Not possible. You haven't seen the place in all its glory. Come on, I'll give you a tour, and George will be thrilled to see you. You have some time?"

"I do."

I followed Ian back up the slope and through the side door, into the warehouse space. Though the outside of the building was nicely finished off, the warehouse wasn't quite done. Even though warehouses weren't supposed to have fancy walls and floors, this big room still had exposed mud patches on the drywall.

"I haven't gotten to the walls because they seem like the least important thing. I got the house done, and then I had orders to fill and lavender oil to make. I'll paint the walls in here at some point but for now you can see that I've split it up into two areas: metalwork and lavender stuff. Well, you can sort of see it. It's kind of a mess but I know where everything is and I'm sure I'll get organized someday." Ian smiled.

I looked at him. He truly had found his passion and was in his element. He'd gone to college for math, but had always wanted to create art. I was genuinely happy for him.

"This is great, Ian," I said as I looked around at the metal scraps and pieces he would turn into interesting shapes that moved with the wind. There were machines that cut or formed the pieces, machines I'd seen him work with but still didn't quite understand. A welder's mask was tipped on its side on one of the tables and there was a slight smell of burnt motor oil in the room. On the other side were two tables that were covered in chemistry-type equipment. Bottles, beakers, and funnels, things that made me think of frog dissections and stinky high school experiments.

"Thanks." He looked around the room. Maybe he was trying to see it through my eyes. If so, he'd be impressed. "How much oil do you need?" He stepped around the chemistry table and reached to a back shelf. "What is your mom making?"

"I think she's baking something. I don't think she'll need much."

"A couple small bottles will probably be okay, but let me know if she needs more than this." He grabbed the brown bottles from a shelf and brought them back around.

"Perfect. What do I owe you?"

"Are you kidding? For your mom? No, we won't charge her today. Maybe down the road, but not today. Come on, let's go find George."

I followed him out of the warehouse and into a hallway between the work and living spaces. This part was more finished, and similar to the outside, the lines inside were simple, yet somehow cozy. The floors were polished walnut and the walls painted off-white. Ian stopped at a closed door and knocked.

"George, you decent?" he said. "We've got company."

"Well, I'm dressed if that's what you mean," George said from the other side of the door. "Come in."

George's studio apartment was one large room with areas devoted to different things like eating, sleeping, and reading. But all the walls except the one that contained the small kitchenette were covered with filled bookshelves. Ian said he'd bring George's library to his new home, and it looked like he'd done exactly that. He'd even brought George's worn and comfortable reading chair and his standing lamp with its fringed shade that had yellowed from time.

"Becca! How delightful," George said when I got close enough that he could see me through his thick glasses. His vision was terrible, but the glasses helped a little. He didn't read much on his own if at all anymore, but listened to recorded books or was read to. I'd read a book or two aloud when he'd lived in his old French Tudor on Harvard, and I was sure Ian still read to him when he could. It had been a big project to gather all the books, but they were his world, and though his apartment was homey, I knew having the books around him had been important.

"George, you look great!" I said as I hugged him.

"That boy keeps feeding me," he said. "I've gained back a

little weight. The doctor is pleased so I guess that's a good thing."

"That's good news," I said.

George had been losing weight before he'd moved to Ian's farm. He'd lost his desire to do much cooking and seemed to forget a few meals. He did look better now with a little more meat on his bones and filled-out cheeks.

"And this creature"—he reached back to the arm of the chair and scratched behind the ears of a very black, very green-eyed, short-haired cat—"keeps me on my toes."

I'd almost run over Magic when she was a tiny newborn kitten. I'd stopped just in time, and though she'd thanked me by digging her claws into my neck, I'd brought her to George. Destiny had taken over and they became quickly smitten with each other.

But I didn't think Magic liked me all that much. As she pushed her head into George's fingers, she looked at me with green-eyed suspicion.

"Hey, Magic," I said. She tipped her head and inspected me, but only for a moment.

"What's the occasion for your visit?" George said.

"Getting lavender for my mom," I said.

"This is the place for that. Ian's farm is becoming quite the spot."

"I agree," I said.

"Come with us to the kitchen, George. Becca hasn't seen that part. I think she'll like it. She likes kitchens."

"Ah, yes, come along, Magic," George said.

I followed behind both Ian and George as we walked

down another short hallway and into Ian's living areas. Magic stayed at my heels, but in that cat way, just far enough behind so she didn't run into them.

Ian's living space was unexpected. It was terrific—no, extra terrific. The great room began at the front of the house with a giant space that held three couches. There was a modern flat-screen television but it was small and looked somewhat neglected on the wide television stand. The space directly behind the couches was filled with a long dark walnut dining table, which was in turn topped with papers, two laptops, and what I thought was some dried lavender. Next was the kitchen island with a few stools tucked under it and a sink at its far end. Along the back wall were the rest of the appliances, surrounded by light blue shelves. The floors were all off-white tile that matched the color on the walls. There was nothing fancy about any of it, but the simplicity suited Ian— modern yet homey.

"It is beautiful," I said. "Just great."

"Thanks," Ian said.

"Look at the view out the windows," George said.

There were five tall windows along the side wall of the house. They framed the lavender field. I moved past the dining table so I could get a better look.

"It's stunning," I said. I'd already noticed that the field looked like something from a Van Gogh. The windows made it a framed masterpiece.

"It is," George said. "I can't see it as well as most people and even I know how wonderful it is."

"I like how it turned out," Ian said. "But what about this kitchen? Isn't it perfect? Too bad I don't do preserves."

I walked back to the kitchen, pretended to give Ian a stern, doubting look (which only made him smile), and then inspected everything as if I wore a white glove.

"Well, it's pretty close to perfect," I said with a wink toward George, though I had no idea if he saw it or not. "No, it's absolutely perfect. Really great, Ian."

"Thanks," Ian said.

George pulled up a stool and said, "Becca, I heard about a death at the bank. You have connections. Was it a murder?"

"I think that's what's been determined."

"Oh, dear. I knew Robert Ship. He was a neighbor and a friend at one time."

I pulled up a stool, too. "He was? A neighbor at the Harvard house?"

"Yes. He was a nice man."

"I'm sorry for your loss then."

"I'm sorry he's gone. Honestly, I can't imagine anyone wanting him dead. He was a quiet man with a quiet life. He worked in the licensing office downtown."

"I know. I was there just this morning. The two people who were working seemed sad about his death."

"I don't know much about his co-workers, but I know he was well liked around the community. We're not a large place, but we have our fair share of businesses. His was not a controversial government job by any stretch of the imagination. Paying for one's business license isn't a big deal, but he was good at reminding people when theirs was about to expire. He took it quite seriously actually."

"Did you ever have your own business license?" I said.

"No," George said.

"Well, you're right in that it's no big deal to keep it active, just a yearly nominal fee. But the first time you apply for one, you have to answer some questions about your past possible involvement in illegal activities, whether you've been convicted of any crime, and if they were felonies on your record. It occurred to me that maybe someone lied on their application and Mr. Ship found out about the lie. Maybe he confronted them."

George thought a moment. "No, I don't think he would have confronted anyone, Becca. It wasn't his style. Now, if he found something illegal, I have no doubt at all that he would have gone to the police. He was very much about doing the right thing."

I didn't want to argue with George, but I'd gotten a different impression from Mr. Ship's co-workers. They'd mentioned that Mr. Ship had let Jeff slide for what I interpreted they deemed was probably too long. I was sure they thought he should have gone to the police much sooner.

"How much of his family do you know?" I asked.

"His wife died many years ago, and he raised their two kids mostly on his own. They left Monson when they went away to college and never moved back, but I'm pretty sure they've always had a friendly relationship."

"Do you know his extended family at all? His niece has—or had, she might not be coming back—a tomato stall at Bailey's. Her name is Betsy."

"Yes, of course. I don't know her well, but there were family events at his house and I think Betsy was there a few times.

Again, I wasn't around them all that much, but I never sensed any problems between any of the family members. The get-togethers were never rowdy in a bad way. But that was a long time ago, Becca. Time moves at such a different pace when you're my age. My past has become compartmentalized into some unexpected categories. I believe Betsy was a young girl when she was at Robert's house. That's still how I think of her."

I nodded. "She's full grown now."

"Yes, then, it has been some time. Has Sam mentioned if the police have any idea about what happened?"

"They're still in the evidence-gathering phase. Some things happened at Bailey's the day before Mr. Ship was killed that probably have nothing to do with his murder, but the police think are notable. When Mr. Ship was at the market to talk to some food truck vendors, he also mentioned a couple market vendors who had issues with their licenses. Betsy's business license had expired and another vendor's had never been purchased. Our baked potato vendor, Jeff, claims that there's a loophole in the law that allows him to operate a food cart without purchasing a business license."

"Really? How long has Jeff had the cart?"

"About a year."

"There's no question that he would be required to have a license, Becca. No matter what he tried to manipulate, if you sell a product, you definitely are required to have a business license. What's he have to say for himself regarding the murder?"

"I haven't seen him. I don't know if Sam has talked to him yet. Jeff hasn't been at the market for two days."

"Hmm," George said. "Well, Jeff's absence might or might not have had anything to do with Robert's murder, but it's a possibility, I guess."

"Jeff's not a bad guy," Ian added. "He keeps to himself, and he's resolutely single, but not terrible. He strikes me as an independent sort, but I can't imagine him not getting a business license."

"I'm surprised Allison allowed Jeff to keep his cart," George added.

"Oh," I said. "I think Jeff told her he was working on things, and even though it's unlike Allison, she never did follow up completely. She's not happy with herself, I'm sure." I paused. "But there is another part to this."

I told Ian and George about Peyton and her behavior and her poor timing regarding the murder. I didn't, however, tell them about Harry's reason for visiting Monson, about my cousin's alleged involvement in the lesser Arizona crimes. I wasn't sure why my gut told me to keep that information to myself, but I always listened to my gut. Besides, somehow her poor timing in Arizona only made her poor timing in South Carolina worse. Maybe I didn't want to pile more problems on.

"Ian mentioned your cousin was visiting. I got the impression he thought she was cute," George said.

Ian's eyes got big as he looked at George. Then he smiled. "Well, I'm not sure that's what I said."

George shrugged. "I could hear it in your voice."

"She's very cute. She's beautiful, actually. And she might have noticed Ian, too," I said without even one small thread of territorial jealousy zipping through me. Yeah, it might be weird if Ian and one of my relatives were to date, but as long as it wasn't my mom or sister, I didn't think it would bother me too much. In fact, the idea of seeing Ian happy was important to me; maybe more important than I'd acknowledged to myself until that very moment.

Of course, at the moment Peyton was a potential thief and killer, so I didn't think now was the time to fix them up.

Nevertheless I said, "You two should join us for dinner at my mom's house."

"Becca, that wasn't obvious at all," Ian said with another smile.

"What do you think, Ian? Should we?" George said.

"As great at it would be to see Becca's family, I have way too much work to do around here. But thanks, you two, for the assistance with my personal life."

"Always here to help," George said. "Thanks for the invite, Becca, but I'll pass, too. I'm tired. A rain check would be great, though."

"Of course."

I left with the lavender oil and a deeper sense of "rightness" in my soul. Yes, our breakup had been difficult—for both of us. And even if ultimately we had been okay together in a long-term, deeper relationship, I had no doubt now that we were going to be able to be real friends. Whatever axis had been off-kilter had now righted itself.

There were so many occasions when grown-up stuff threw me for a loop; it was nice to feel a sense of maturity without panic over whether or not I'd done the right thing.

Of course, choosing the correct path wasn't always my

strong suit, I thought as I turned the opposite direction I was supposed to go to get to my parents' house. I was going to be late, I decided. Maybe since everything had been so effortless at Ian's, I had the need to do something risky, something that might send me down the wrong path.

Thirteen

Bailey's was open on Friday and Saturday nights until about nine during the summer and early fall. But tonight, Wednesday, everything shut down at around six, and like most evenings when Bailey's shut down, it really shut down. Quitting time, if selling out of product for the day hadn't occurred earlier, was a welcome moment for vendors who not only spent their days outside at the market, but also spent lots of time tending their crops or making their products. Farmers' market work was physical, and wasn't for sissies. Being done for the day held a great sense of satisfaction, as well as a moment to know that a well-earned rest was hopefully soon to come.

I'd come back to the market after it had closed a time or two over the years. I'd needed to pick up a forgotten item, or fix a display table, or replace one. It happened. It was an open air market. Though there were tent walls, there was a sense that the stalls were all part of one single, really big place. There were no doors except on the small building that housed Allison's office. Anyone or any creature could walk through the market at any time. We'd all experienced a surprise cat or dog, or chicken for that matter, there to greet us as we unloaded in the morning.

I didn't like being on the market grounds at night; there were no nearby streetlights and it was too dark once the lighted sign in the parking lot was powered down. Currently the sun hadn't quite set all the way and the stalls, parking lot, and food trucks were all bathed in a murky glow that seemed peaceful, if not eerie.

The food trucks were shut tight, silent soldiers lined up along the edge of the parking lot. My truck was the only other vehicle in sight, and when my headlights hit the food trucks, they seemed more like they were lurking and waiting for me, rather than just parked. My imagination sprouted and I could visualize the trucks coming to life as I slowly approached them.

I laughed at myself and shook off the willies.

"All right, Peyton, let's see what you were up to," I said as I parked and repeated to myself that they were only trucks, not creatures in a science fiction book or movie.

However, once I turned the key and my truck was as silent as the others, I had to fight a chill up my spine.

"Oh, for goodness' sake," I muttered as I opened the door and got out.

I moved to almost the same spot I'd seen Basha standing in and stared up at the side panel of Peyton's truck, at the corner. I even put my hands on my hips, mimicking Basha's pose. There wasn't much light left, but when I looked hard, I thought I might be seeing something. Maybe.

Along the top and back edge of the panel was a pipe— could be a tube. Again, maybe. At the top corner, there was a cap over the pipe. I only noticed the cap because it wasn't on straight.

"Did you put something in there?" I said.

I looked around. I knew there was a ladder in Allison's office, but I didn't want to disturb the key on the top of the door frame and let myself in. There were probably other ladders on the market premises, but I wasn't going to search for them. I jumped into my truck, maneuvered the bed up next to the back corner of Peyton's. I grabbed the flashlight out of my glove box and scurried up the side of my truck's bed, ultimately balancing one foot on the side and one on the tailgate. I was short but from there I could reach the cap. I held the flashlight in my armpit as I used one hand to hold me up and one to yank off the cap. It came off easily, almost too easily. I teetered, but rebalanced quickly.

I grabbed the flashlight and aimed it inside the pipe, which confirmed that it was, in deed, a hollow tube. I saw nothing. Well, not much of anything, at least. There were some small clumps of dirt, but nothing else; no rolled-up treasure map or diary page with a confession of crimes committed, like I'd hoped to find. I thought the dirt could be from the bag I'd seen Peyton with, but dirt was dirt, for the most part.

"This is dumb," I said to the open mouth of the tube. I put the flashlight under my arm and reached to return the cap to its spot.

"What're you doing?" a voice said from somewhere to my right.

I screamed and lost my balance. My feet slipped and the rest of me fell toward the voice as the cap and the flashlight flew in other undetermined directions.

I assumed the voice was attached to the arms that caught me. I landed in them much more gracefully than I thought I was capable of doing.

"You okay?" It was Mel, of Paco's Tacos.

"I'm fine. I'm sorry. Thanks, though, for being quick enough to keep me from falling," I said as I squirmed out of his arms.

"No problem," he said as his now empty hands moved to his hips. "What were you doing up there?"

"It's a long story." I wiped my hands on my shorts. "What are you doing here?"

"Actually, I was, well, we were getting ready to pull out a deck of cards."

"I don't understand."

"Hank, Daryl, and I just finished cleaning up our trucks. We were going to play a game of cards before we went to the hotel."

I looked at the trucks and then at Mel. "Where are you playing cards? I didn't see any of you."

"Hank and Daryl are on the other side setting up the card table. You're Becca, right?"

"I am. I make and sell jams and preserves."

"Right. We've talked. You were helping Peyton earlier. And you're Peyton's cousin?"

"I am."

Mel rubbed his chin as he looked at me a long moment and then back up at Peyton's truck. "I have time for a story if you'd like to tell me what's going on."

"I think I'd better tell my cousin first. Maybe catch me tomorrow, but thanks a bunch for catching me *tonight*." I smiled.

Mel smiled back and then looked at me for another long, awkward moment. His surfer dude persona contradicted whatever seemed to be going on behind his eyes. I couldn't be sure if he was thinking or plotting, but something was happening in there.

I turned to gather the flashlight from the truck bed so I could search for the pipe cap.

"Hey," Mel said. "About Peyton. I don't want to seem creepy, but do you know if she's single? She's . . . she's very pretty, and I thought about asking her out, but if she's got a boyfriend, you could save me from embarrassing myself too much."

"I honestly don't know," I said as I pulled out the flashlight and shined it on the ground around us. "You could ask her, though. It never hurts to ask."

I didn't know one thing about Peyton's love life other than the bad choice she'd made to follow a guy to Arizona. I didn't know the types of guys she was interested in, except for Ian, but he's intriguing even if he doesn't fit a type. The only things I knew about Mel were that he was good with tacos, he had sharp reflexes, and he'd seemed helpful with the generators.

"Sure. She's a little different," he said.

"How do you mean?" I swung the light up to his face but pulled it away when he lifted his hand to shield his eyes.

"I saw you spying on her back there the other day." He nodded toward the grass patch. "I guess I was spying, too. Or I was just curious about what you were up to. I saw you crouch and then watch her come out the back of her truck for a second. Does what you were doing tonight have anything to do with that?"

"No," I said. Either I could ask him more questions about what he saw or thought he saw or how he happened to see what he thought he saw, or I could get out of there and hurry to my parents' late dinner, which was now really late. I opted for the last choice.

Mel nodded. "Just wondered." He looked up at the truck again. "Did you figure out what was going on, back there, I mean?"

"No. Did you?"

"No, but I didn't ask her. I thought it was none of my business, and like I said, I think she's pretty. I didn't want to scare her away or anything."

I heard a hint of amusement in his voice but I wasn't sure what kind of amusement it was; did he find something funny or was he trying to be clever?

I shined the light on the ground again. I found the cap next to my rear tire. I grabbed it and put it in my pocket. I decided I would give Peyton the cap at dinner and tell her what I'd been up to. I'd also mention that both Mel and I had seen her behaving "curiously." It was time to get some answers.

"Want to join us?" Mel said. "For cards?"

"You're really going to play here?"

"Yeah, why not? It's a beautiful night and none of us want to be stuck in our hotel rooms yet."

"Makes sense," I said. "No thanks, though. I need to get going."

"See you tomorrow," Mel said. He lifted his hand and waved before turning and disappearing through the space between Peyton's and his trucks.

I was curious enough about the nighttime card game that once he was out of sight, I followed his path and peeked carefully around to the backside. True to his word, he, Hank, and Daryl were seated around a card table with a battery-powered lantern on top.

"Everything okay?" Hank asked Mel.

"Yeah, just a market worker."

"Really? This time of night?"

"I know. Weird. She's Peyton's cousin."

"Oh," Hank said as if Mel's explanation adequately explained what was going on. "I wonder if Peyton is single."

"I wondered the same thing."

"Gentlemen," Daryl said. "We're traveling food truck chefs. We're not traveling salesmen. 'The road ain't no place to start a family'—to quote from one of the best bands of all time."

"Good point," Mel said.

But there was something in the way that Hank remained silent. My eyes were drawn to him. Both Mel and Daryl looked at him, too, as if they also expected a comment.

He finally spoke. "I don't know, she's pretty. But maybe

'I'm just talkin' 'bout tonight'—to quote from one of the best country singers of all time."

Mel and Daryl laughed.

I didn't need to hear more, so I slipped backward through the slot and got into my truck.

Suddenly, I couldn't wait to talk to Peyton. She had a right to know that I'd spied on her. I would tell her tonight at my parents' house. I would tell her everything, and maybe she'd do the same with me.

Fourteen

Unfortunately, Peyton wasn't at my parents' house. Neither were
Allison; her husband, Tom; or their son, Mathis. The best
that my mom could interpret from Allison's call was that
Peyton wasn't feeling well and Allison didn't think it was
fair to leave her alone.

I didn't tell my parents my own interpretation, which
was: whatever the reason for Peyton not wanting to go out,
Allison didn't trust her enough to leave her alone. Allison
probably gave Peyton the impression that she was being a
supportive family member, but I was sure Peyton was being
watched closely.

Although Allison would have a level of patience with
Peyton that I probably wouldn't have, so there was a chance

my sister actually was just being supportive and I was the only suspicious one.

Since Peyton wasn't going to be joining us, I called Sam and invited him and Harry. I hadn't heard about the dinner until midafternoon, and since the subject of both of their investigations—Peyton—was supposed to be there, Sam and I had agreed that he shouldn't join in the fun. Both he and Harry were pleased with the change of plans. They arrived only a short time later, and they brought Hobbit.

My parents were always delighted to meet new people. Even if this one was investigating their niece because of potential criminal activity, they were still willing to welcome him to their home and give him a full dose of Polly and Jason Robins.

Somehow they were able to dish out the third degree without the person on the receiving end figuring out what was going on or later becoming offended by what had happened. My parents liked to get to know people on a level a few floors deeper than the surface. They were fascinated by what made other people tick, deep down inside.

When I was younger, I'd never given them the credit they probably deserved for their keen intelligence. They were hippies, and hippies weren't supposed to be smart, were they? Polly and Jason Robins were a couple of smart hippies.

Even though they'd participated in more rallies and causes than I could remember, they were different one-on-one, with a need to understand other people and other views before sharing their own. They didn't argue and they didn't try to change minds . . . one-on-one. In front of a building that had what they deemed questionable business practices going on inside and with arms loaded with signs while singing clever chants, oh yeah, you bet they'd try to change minds. But never one-on-one.

And they never used any sort of persuasive pressure on a visitor in their home. Put simply, they thought that was bad manners. They were people people—all kinds of people people.

"How hard was it to leave the reservation?" Mom asked Harry as she handed him a glass of lemonade that she'd squeezed herself. She'd also baked a platter full of sugar cookies for our casual dessert. The lavender oil had been for frosting the cookies. She explained that oil was much better than extract when it came to adding flavor to icing or frosting. I doubted I'd ever attempt to make lavender frosting, but I hoped she'd continue to put it on her sugar cookies.

It was only about a year ago that my parents had come off the road after a two-year RV trip. They'd moved into one of the smaller homes they owned in town. They owned quite a few Monson area houses, which they rented out, but they wouldn't tell Allison or me exactly how many. This one was cute and the perfect size for two people who didn't need a lot of space. Dad had just built a wooden shade awning for the small back patio, and with it the evening was again comfortable enough to enjoy outside.

"The most difficult part for my family, and for those who I consider my family but aren't true blood relatives—we're all family on the reservation—was that I wasn't going to be a reservation law officer. I'm a county officer. That was hard for them to accept, but the adjustment has mostly been made. My older sister still has issues with me." Harry laughed.

"But I've never quite lived up to her expectations. I was supposed to be an artist."

"What type of artist?" Mom asked.

"Beading. Jewelry."

"Are you good at it?"

"Not anymore. I used to be. When I hit about forty-five, the eyesight started to get in the way and my fingers became much less nimble."

"Sounds like you made the right career choice," Dad said.

"I love my job," Harry said. "Even when it might come in between friendships. I know that Peyton is your niece."

Mom blinked. "You know, I don't think Peyton is capable of committing a crime, but she's just flighty enough not to think through her actions sometimes. Only the evidence will tell, but I have every confidence that she will be exonerated."

"I hope so," Harry said sincerely.

"Now, Sam, what can you tell us about Robert Ship's murder? It's so terribly tragic," Mom said.

"Yes, it is. And unfortunately, Polly, I can't tell you much. No one saw anything and there doesn't seem to be a lot of evidence. We're working on it."

"Did you know that Betsy, the tomato lady from the market, was Robert Ship's niece?" I said. "Harry and I found out when we went to visit her."

"I did know that," Mom said. "But, of course, I know the whole family. Or knew them. I guess we used to be friends, but that was a few years back. Nothing happened to break the friendship. Lives just go in different directions. They were a fun group of people when we knew them, and very earthy. They all had farms or gardens. I heard that Betsy's father, Nick, Robert's brother, built a house that uses only solar power, which is impressive. Dad and I have thought lots about solar power," Mom said.

"We have. I'm sure we'll do something with it in the next year or so," Dad said. "We're just not sure exactly what."

I knew that Harry had told Sam about our visit with Betsy, and I'd given Sam the glove I'd stolen. I told him it might have Betsy's fingerprints inside just in case he thought they would need them. I asked him not to ask me how I got it and he'd obliged. I looked at him now to see if I could read whether or not learning about Mr. Ship's brother was of interest, but his expression didn't tell me anything.

"Do you know if they all still get along?" I said to Mom.

"Gosh, I'm not sure about recent relations. I know there was a problem with the solar panels Nick used, and Robert, being a city employee, thought it was his job to bring the issue to a town meeting. Ultimately the vote went in Nick's direction. I don't think Robert was upset about the end result, although he might have been, I suppose." Mom thought a minute. "I don't know. I don't remember any bad feelings, but before the vote, Robert was pretty determined that Nick was breaking the law, big time. There was mention of 'clauses and articles' but the town council didn't see things the same way Robert did. Yes, Robert might have been embarrassed."

Sam and Harry exchanged a look. What had my mom said that caused the look?

"I understand the Arizona difficulties, Harry, but you and Sam don't really think that Peyton could have killed Robert Ship?" Dad asked.

Neither of them said anything for a very long moment,

too long. I'd hoped for a quick, confident, and comforting answer in the negative.

"We don't have much of anything pointing us to anyone," Sam said.

I looked at Harry, whose expression was also unreadable, a stern poker face.

"Harry?" I said.

"I don't know, Becca. I still have strong feelings that it's Peyton on the video. And the money is either missing or what was used to purchase the food truck. I don't know if she could have killed anyone."

I swallowed. Had the money been something she stuck into the pipe? No, that amount of money would have taken up more space than the space in the pipe would have allowed, or the canvas bag I'd seen her with, for that matter. My imagination was sprouting again, this time sprinkled with fear and concern for her.

"Can we see the video?" Mom asked.

"Sure." Harry pulled his phone from his pocket. A few seconds later, we'd huddled around him and he'd expanded the picture to fill the small but visible screen.

"That's not Peyton," Mom said when it was over.

"What makes you so sure?" Harry said.

"Two reasons. I'm sure she's not nearly strong enough for that, and her curls aren't that perfect. That's a wig. However, I wouldn't be surprised if it was someone trying to look like Peyton. Yes, I'm sure that's not her."

"Play it again," I said, repeating the same request I'd made at the police station.

As the video played again, I realized my mom was correct. Peyton's curls weren't nearly that perfect. In fact, no one's real curls were that perfect. Only a wig had such flawless curls.

"I think you're right, Mom," I said when the video had played two more times.

"Of course she is," Dad said proudly.

"You have a point," Harry admitted as he studied the screen again.

I got the distinct impression that Harry did agree that my mom *might* be correct, but he was also considering other contingencies. Perhaps the small screen only made the curls look so perfect, or . . . or whatever other contingencies law enforcement people took into consideration.

"All right then, Harry, tell us about the adventure in Arizona with Becca. She told us what happened, but I'm sure she left out some of the scarier parts. I'd like to know them now. Plenty of time has passed. I think we can handle the truth," Mom said.

Harry put his phone back into his pocket and shot me a brief reassuring glance that told me he would still leave out some of the events that had transpired. He knew that even parents who'd had enough time and knew their child was fine still couldn't always handle the whole scary truth.

True to the glance, he left out the worst parts of the story, but kept enough in so that my parents thought they were getting all the gory details.

After we all said good night, Harry took his rental back to Sam's, and Sam drove me and Hobbit home in my truck.

I hadn't realized I was so tired until Sam had to lift my groggy, half-asleep body from the passenger side to deposit me into bed. I didn't remember anything after that.

Until my phone rang and buzzed loud enough to wake the dead. Well, almost.

Fifteen

"*Becca, are you coming into the market today?*" I was pretty sure it was Peyton's voice on the other end of the phone, but it was tight and breathy.

I looked at the dark window and then reached over to the other side of the bed. It was still a little warm. With the noise coming from the bathroom, I deduced that Sam was in the shower.

"What time is it, Peyton?"

"About five thirty."

"Well," I said as I wearily sat up, "yes, I'm coming in, but it's a little early."

"Really? There are other vendors setting up and Allison just got us here."

I'd cursed my sister's perfection more than a few times

over the years, but my biggest issue was with her need to always be so on time. I'd tried to change her, but to no avail.

"Right," I said. "You need me to come in?"

"Yes, right away if possible."

"Give me a few and I'll be there. You okay?"

"Yes, I just need to talk to you about something," Peyton said.

"I'll be there soon."

After I ended the call, my muddy brain solidified a little more. It wasn't unusual that Sam got up early, but normally he would go work out and then shower at his house. Sometimes he got ready at my house, but those days were rare. I didn't have time to catch up and ask about it because his exit was hurried and his farewell was distracted.

After my own shower and some big gulps of coffee, I hurried Hobbit through her morning routine and then I tried to call Sam to see what was up, but he didn't answer. Another bad sign.

Once Hobbit was taken care of, the sun was beginning to come up and I'd gotten rid of most of the sleep cobwebs.

My truck went only so fast even when I floored it, so though I was now in a real hurry to get to Peyton, I wasn't going to be in danger of breaking speed limit laws.

I arrived at the back entrance of my stall earlier than I had in a long time. Most farm people, most of the farmers' market folks, too, were morning people and woke up early naturally, particularly the old-timers, those who'd been farming for their whole lives. On those rare occasions when I was at the market before an old-timer or two, I was boosted with temporary confidence and the hope that I might be like them someday.

I moved through the back wall of my stall with the plan to drop off one box and then go find Peyton out in the parking lot. But she surprised me and was sitting on my front display table when I came through.

"Need help?" she said as she hopped off the table.

"Sure. No, wait." I looked at the box of jams I was holding. "Do we need to talk?"

"I'd like to."

She didn't want a casual conversation; that was obvious.

"Let's go to your truck. These are just canvas walls," I said.

"Good plan."

I put the box on a chair and we made our way out of the market.

"Did you want Allison in on this? Did you talk to her already?" I asked as we passed her office.

"No, I didn't. She's so busy, Becca. I don't want to bother her."

I nodded. I wasn't bothered, and I got what she was saying—Allison was always busy. While she would have easily lent an ear to Peyton, it was better this way.

We exited the market and walked over the empty parking lot. Basha's cupcake truck was open, the counter door lifted up, and I could see the cupcake baker inside holding a pastry bag over a cupcake tin.

"Hi, Basha," I said as we passed by her truck.

She looked up. "Ladies," she said in greeting. There was

a small question to her tone, but I waved as if to let her know everything was fine.

She turned back to the cupcake tin.

"I don't think she likes me," Peyton said quietly.

"Why?"

"Probably everything."

I nodded. Hard to argue with that one.

Peyton came around to the passenger side first, unlocked the door, and waited until I was inside before she shut the door and walked around to the driver's side.

"The police called Allison this morning. They asked her to bring me into the station," she said when she was settled inside.

I blinked, Sam's morning departure now made a little more sense, but there were still lots of missing pieces.

"Did you go? How early? What happened?" I said.

"I didn't go. Allison told the police that she could take me in around seven o'clock but that she had a conference call before then. She"—Peyton paused as if she was trying not to cry—"told them they could pick me up at her house or at the market."

I put my hand on her arm. "She didn't have any choice, Peyton."

"I know, but . . . we're related, Becca. It hurt."

"Did you want her to tell them no or to hide you? Allison couldn't do that, you know that, don't you? It's better for you this way, too."

"I do, but still . . . anyway," she sniffed, "they told her that they have some evidence they want to talk to me about."

"Okay, well, that might not be so bad. Right? Just talk."

I hoped she didn't see me swallow hard. They had evidence? That was new.

She shook her head, causing her dark curls to bounce in such a little girl way that my heart hurt for her. But she wasn't a little girl. She was a woman who should be old enough to make good choices.

"Peyton, it's okay. Let me call Sam." I pulled out my phone, punched the button to call, and hoped he'd answer.

"Becca?" he said.

"Hey, Sam. Do you need to see Peyton?" I said.

"I do. I'm just about to leave the station and head out to the market. Where are you?"

"At the market, with Peyton. We're sitting in her food truck. She's nervous, Sam. Can you tell me what this is about?"

I wanted him to tell me that it was no big deal, that he just needed to talk to her briefly. That she would be fine. But he hesitated before he said anything. I knew that hesitation—it wasn't usually followed by good news.

"I do just need to chat with her briefly," Sam said. Even though it was what I wanted to hear, I knew he was lying. There was something big going on, and there would be nothing brief about their conversation.

"Okay," I said. "Sounds good. We'll wait right here."

"Be there in a minute."

I disconnected the call, put my phone back in my pocket, and hoped I hid my concern.

"Sounds like it's no biggie, Peyton. Let's just wait and talk to Sam. He's very reasonable."

"Becca, I haven't done anything wrong. I'm innocent of . . . everything."

"Okay."

"I need to get out of here." Peyton started the truck.

"Wait a sec. No, this isn't a good idea. Where are you going to go?" I said as the engine revved.

"I'm not sure. We're close to the ocean. Maybe I can get out of the country." She backed the truck and then pulled it away from the line.

I laughed, but my cousin was being one hundred percent serious. She wasn't thinking clearly.

"No, we're not going to do that. Stop the truck," I said.

But she didn't stop the truck. Instead she sped up through the parking lot, and then pulled the truck out to the two-lane highway, turning the steering wheel so forcefully that one side of the truck lifted off the ground momentarily.

"This isn't safe," I said.

"Hang on, Becca. Hang on tight."

Sixteen

DONE RUNNING

The journey off the road and down the small berm was bumpy and too wild for my tastes. Both Peyton and I were knocked around enough to end up with small cuts on our faces (oddly in the same spots on our right cheeks, though we had no idea how we got them) and plenty of bruises and sore muscles that wouldn't hit full force for a day or two.

Neither of us lost consciousness, which I thought was a good thing. I didn't hit my head and she didn't think she had hit hers.

"That was one of the dumbest things I've ever seen," I said when I was sure we were both okay enough for me to get mad.

"I know. I'm sorry," she said. "Really, really sorry."

I sighed and realized that neither of us had been buckled

in. It was an odd moment to notice such a thing, but it's where my attention went. At least until I heard the approaching siren.

"I'm sorry," Peyton said again, her voice lined with complete defeat and the certain approach of tears. "Becca, I don't think I'm going to get out of this okay. I really do think someone is trying to frame me. But it's important for me to tell you that I am innocent."

I looked at her a long moment. She didn't look like a little girl anymore, but she was still my little cousin, the one Allison and I had gotten into more trouble than we should have. She was family. And I believed, in that deep-gut-feeling, I-just-know way, that she was telling me the truth. I hoped she was.

"Then we'll figure it out," I said.

A second later, Sam was at the passenger door of the truck, and Officer Vivienne Norton was opening the driver's side door. She yanked Peyton out of the truck.

I opened my door. "I'm fine," I said to Sam.

We'd been pretty good about keeping our public displays of affection to a minimum, particularly when he was on duty. I didn't think he currently cared who was watching as he put his finger to my chin and turned my face toward him.

"You're really okay?" he said, his icy blue eyes both intense and scared.

"I'm fine. Not hurt."

He helped me out of the truck and inspected my face again. I didn't know he carried a handkerchief but one appeared, seemingly from his back pocket, and he dabbed at the cut.

"It's not deep. No stitches," he said.

"That's a first," I said with a laugh.

He smiled briefly and then pulled me into a hug that was so close I thought he might never let me go, and I was okay with it.

I could hear his fast heartbeat and feel his strong arms locked around me.

"Becca," he muttered, but I didn't think he was talking to me.

"I'm fine. Totally."

He kissed the top of my head but still didn't let go. "I know. I know."

Sam and I had been in a hairy situation or two, and a few years earlier, long before we'd met, he'd lost his fiancée to a tragedy, something for which he blamed himself. I knew that he'd tried not to be overprotective of me. No, that wasn't it. He'd tried very hard to *hide* his overprotectiveness. I didn't know if he was currently overreacting or not, but I figured it was best just to ride out the moment. Plus, he smelled really good, like soap and laundry detergent, topped off with a slight peppermint-y wave of that mystery gunk he put in his hair. And his strong arms were so comfortable.

It was only Peyton's scream for help that took me out of the moment. When she yelled my name, I pushed back from Sam and ran around the truck. He was right behind me.

"Peyton!" I said as I ran toward her.

Officer Norton had my cousin, my now grown-up cousin who was once cute and little and who'd always been sweet and kind, down on the ground on her belly. Officer Norton had her knee on Peyton's backside and had pulled her wrists behind her back, securing them with steely handcuffs.

"Step back, Ms. Robins, or you'll be interfering with police business," Officer Norton said. Her voice was calm and even, but she still somehow managed to instill fear into me.

"Becca," Sam said as he put his hand on my arm and ever so slightly pulled me back.

"Sam?"

He nodded and then turned his attention to Vivienne. "Viv, here, let me help."

In one quick, almost flight-like movement, the two of them lifted Peyton to a standing position.

"Are you hurt, Ms. Chase?" Sam said as he inspected Peyton's face with almost the same intensity that he'd inspected mine, but only with concern, no deep fear for her.

"That beast of a woman might have ripped my arms out of my sockets, but I'm okay."

"Good. All right, we're going to get you and Becca to a doctor to make sure you're all right but I need to . . ." Sam looked at me briefly. There was no apology in those icy eyes. "Peyton Chase, you are under arrest for the murder of Robert Ship . . ."

The rest of everything Sam said was lost in the ocean noises filling my head. He was reading my cousin her rights. She was being arrested for murder. Murder. And all the while, waves pounded my ears and crashed around in my head. I didn't want to process what he was really saying.

A few seconds later, another police cruiser pulled up and another officer joined us. I didn't know him, but as I watched his long legs move down the berm, he reminded me of a grasshopper. Sam instructed the grasshopper officer and Vivienne to transport Peyton to the doctor and then back to a cell at the small downtown police station.

When the other cruiser had sped away with Peyton's fearful glance out the back window eating at me, Sam directed me to the passenger side of his car.

"What about her truck?" I said.

"I've got some people coming out to take care of it."

"Okay," I said. "Where are we going?"

"My house."

"Sounds good."

I'd only recently learned that Sam had also been trained as an EMT. When we got to his house, he sat me on the couch and gathered his cache of medical instruments. He gave me a concussion test and checked my vitals.

"Not exactly the way we should get to play doctor, is it?" I flirted.

Fortunately, he'd already determined that I was fine, so he could truly smile this time, the concern and fear now mostly gone from his eyes.

He took the stethoscope out of his ears. "I love you, Becca."

I blinked with surprise. "I love you, too."

He smiled at me again, but this time it was a sideways, all-knowing smile. I liked it when he did that, but it always made me wonder what I was missing.

"What?" I said.

"You're adorable," he said. "And it seems you're just fine physically. You don't even need a Band-Aid."

"You're adorable, too."

He cleaned the cut one more time, and then put some antibacterial cream on it.

"Good as new, and still adorable," he said.

"Thank you."

He leaned in for a kiss. It was a quick one, but not without promise.

"See, there's a little doctor play right there," I said, still flirting badly but trying.

This time he laughed. "As wonderful as that sounds right now, I wouldn't feel right if I didn't first let you know that your cousin was arrested under my orders."

"Oh. Okay, well, that must mean you have some strong evidence." I swallowed hard. I did not want that to be the truth.

"We have some evidence," he said as he leaned back into the couch, his medical bag still open on the coffee table in front of us.

"Care to tell me what it is?" I said.

He looked at me, his mouth straightening sharply, and he said, "We have a handwritten recipe card. Harry confirmed with the owners of the restaurant in Arizona where Peyton worked that it's their recipe card. He was up early this morning talking to them. That's why I left so early myself."

I nodded. "Wait. Okay, I know enough of the story to know that Peyton was accused of stealing a recipe from the restaurant, though I didn't visualize a handwritten recipe on a card. Anyway, where did you find the card that makes you think she killed Robert Ship?"

"It was on him. It was in his hand."

"What?"

"We didn't pay a bit of attention to it initially, but the medical examiner finally called us late last night to ask if we wanted the card back. He didn't think it was important at first, but then thought he should ask."

"In Robert Ship's hand?"

"Yes."

"Well, that could mean . . . I have absolutely no idea what that could mean, but it doesn't necessarily mean that Peyton killed him."

"True, but how else would he have gotten the recipe? He must have somehow gotten it from her."

"Taken it from her truck? I don't know, but I don't think she put it in his hand after she killed him, and I can't see how he was holding it before he was killed."

Sam shrugged. "You're right and the particulars are yet to be worked out, but it's a solid piece of evidence."

"Is it all you really have?"

"It's the best we have."

"Then it really isn't much, is it?" I cleared my throat. I hadn't meant to sound so snotty.

"Becca, I'm sorry, but between what Harry's got and what we've got, I think it's only a matter of time before Peyton confesses—though I'm not sure of all the things she'll be confessing to. She got caught up in stuff she couldn't handle and she doesn't have a criminal mind. Her, uh, goodness will come through and she'll spill the beans any minute now."

"What about what my mom said about the curls?"

"I think your mom is right about curls being too perfect, but the video just isn't good enough to trust that that's what we're seeing, perfect curls."

I nodded and thought about Peyton's insistence that she was innocent.

"Sam, you don't think Harry is framing her?"

It was Sam's turn to blink. "Not at all."

"I know, that was a long shot, but when Peyton talked to me, she was adamant that she was innocent. She's sure she's being framed, Sam."

"Lots of guilty people say that."

"I know, but . . . she's *so* sure," I said.

"She's family, Becca. It's hard when family's done something wrong."

"You sound sure that she's guilty," I said.

Sam gave me a level look. "No, I'm a firm believer in innocent until proven guilty, but things aren't looking great. I want you to know that, and I want you to know that I have to do my job even if your family is involved."

"What if it was me? What if I was in Peyton's shoes?" The questions jumped out of me. On some level, I knew what I was doing. I was making myself mad at Sam. It was a bad play, but I couldn't stop myself.

"You're not a killer, nor a thief."

"But what if I got caught up in something that was over my head? Would you arrest me?"

Sam opened his mouth to speak, but then closed it again. He was a by-the-books kind of guy. Of course he would arrest me.

"Becca, you have to know that I would do everything in my power to help and protect you."

That wasn't exactly the answer I was looking for, but I was also extra touchy at the moment.

"Will you do everything in your power to help and protect Peyton?" I said after I took a deep breath.

"Yes," he said.

I was surprised that I didn't believe him. I looked hard at

those icy eyes and wondered what was really going on behind them. I knew it was a tricky situation, considering he and I were practically living together and he was convinced that someone I cared deeply about, a family member, was guilty of heinous crimes. I didn't envy his position, but I wasn't sure I wanted to discuss it with him further at the moment.

"Can you take me back to the market?" I said.

"Becca . . ."

"I'm fine, Sam. I just need to get to work. You need to get back to work, too, don't you?"

"Sure."

There were no apologies from either of us on the trip back to Bailey's, but there were no apologies needed. It was just a sticky situation, that's all. We'd get through it. I hoped.

"Thanks for taking care of me," I said when he stopped outside the Bailey's entrance.

"Always," he said. "This isn't what I want, but I think it's the right thing to do. It's . . . it's only because I don't think we should do anything to compromise Peyton or the ongoing investigation into the crimes that have been committed. But I'll stay at my house for now. It's best for you, too, Becca."

"That makes sense." It did, but I still didn't like it. He didn't like it, either. I was happy to see that in his chameleon eyes.

"I love you, Becca," he said again.

"Love you, too," I said. And then I got out of the car way too fast. I wanted to kick myself, but there was no fixing that particular moment. I'd just have to do better next time.

Almost too gently, Sam pulled the cruiser away and steered it out of the parking lot.

"We'll be okay," I said to myself. I believed it. I had to.

I also believed that I was going to have to get help elsewhere. No matter what Sam thought, I'd looked into my cousin's eyes when she was proclaiming her innocence. And I'd looked into those eyes many years earlier when she said she hadn't stolen the last chocolate chip cookie, and I knew she had lied. A cookie wasn't in the same league as assault, murder, and theft, but I'd seen her lies and her truths, and I was convinced I knew the difference, then and now.

I marched to Allison's office and pushed through her door.

Seventeen

"I can't believe she was really arrested," Allison said. "When Officer Norton called me this morning, I was under the impression that they just wanted to talk to her."

I shook my head.

"All right. Well, of course, I'm here to help, and Mom and Dad will do whatever we ask, I have no doubt." She closed the folder on her desk. She hadn't looked at its contents since I'd burst into her office, but closing it was her way of cementing that she was ready to roll with me, wherever that might take us.

"I was wondering. I'd like to find Robert's brother, Betsy's dad, Nick. Betsy left in such a flurry and Mom mentioned their difficulties. I don't even think Sam and the other officers are looking at him. I think they're pretty convinced that it's all Peyton, but I do think there are other avenues to explore."

Allison's eyebrows came together. "They're good police officers, Becca. Sam's one of the best I've ever seen. They aren't being tunnel-visioned, I'm sure. Sam just didn't feel like he could tell you all the details. It makes sense and it's something you need to come to terms with. He's the police officer, you're the nosy jam maker and market worker."

"Right." I didn't feel like coming to terms with it at that exact moment, though. Maybe tomorrow if I got all my questions answered today. "Want to come with me to find Nick?"

"I do," she said unequivocally. Despite the lecture, she was still ready to roll.

I gathered the box of jams from the chair in my stall and put it back in my truck. Then I grabbed the box of preordered items and asked Linda if she wouldn't mind taking care of them for me. She didn't. She never did. I owed her big.

I left a note on my front counter and Allison and I jumped into my truck. The air-conditioning in her Subaru worked better than my air-conditioning, but neither of us even considered not taking my old, bright orange truck. It was like Shaggy's Mystery Machine at that point, I supposed.

"They live out on Orchard," Allison said after she disconnected the call to our mom. "The solar house is way down the road, at the very end, she thinks."

"Got it," I said.

Orchard Street wasn't located in town. In fact, it was way, way out of town, or at least by about fifteen minutes. Allison and I spent the travel time catching up on family matters. I learned that Mathis had tested (though she detested the "ridiculous" amount of tests he had to take in his preschool setting) very high in math and had grown probably another whole inch since I'd seen him a month earlier. Her husband, Tom, was doing well and had been training to run a marathon. She also said that Mom and Dad told her they thought they were done for good living the RV life and would probably stick around Monson. I hadn't heard that good news yet.

I told her Hobbit was doing great.

As I turned onto Orchard, Allison checked her phone. "Not much service out here."

"Wow, I would never have thought to check my reception *before* I was driving toward someone who might be even a little bit suspicious. You're much better at this than I am," I teased.

"Let's just say we have different strengths. Hang on." She typed something into the phone. "There, I let Tom know where we were headed and to send out a search party in a couple hours if he doesn't hear from me."

"Very impressive."

"I've always been the careful twin, Becca, but that doesn't mean I had the most fun."

I laughed.

Orchard was a narrow dirt road that was lined with tall trees on either side. The crooked sign that told us where we were said "Orchard Road" not "Orchard Street." I didn't know the difference.

"There are no houses out here," I said. "You sure Mom said Orchard?"

"Pretty sure. Just keep driving."

The road was so uneven that I couldn't go very fast, which only a second later turned out to be a good thing.

Suddenly, a deer emerged from the trees and stepped out into the middle of the road. I slammed on the brakes, but it was just simple reaction. I wasn't going fast enough to have hit him, and fortunately, I wasn't going fast enough to propel us through the windshield as I floored the brakes.

"You okay?" I said to Allison.

"Fine, you?"

"Yeah. He's something, isn't he?"

"Beautiful."

The buck was huge with a ten-point rack that reminded me of an insurance company's logo. He looked to be in great shape, with no mars on his coat and no ribs showing around his middle. He stood there and looked at us a long time, but I didn't get the sense that it was the typical deer-in-the-headlights vacant stare. He was considering us.

"I don't really want to honk, but you should go," I said as I shooed him with my hand.

I was pretty sure he raised his eyebrows at me before he turned around and started walking forward.

"Off the road," I said.

He stopped, turned and looked at us, and then seemed to signal us forward with a small swing of his heavy head.

Allison and I looked at each other.

"No way," we said together.

Nevertheless, I put the truck in gear and started to slowly follow the buck. He didn't go too fast or too slow, but meandered, the shade from the thick trees putting everything in a darkish tunnel of sorts.

"Is this happening?" Allison said.

"Looks like it."

The buck stopped at a fork in the road and turned to look at us again.

"We're right here," I said, though I held back waving.

"This is interesting," Allison said.

The buck took the left fork and then glanced behind one more time to make sure we were following. We were.

The bumpy road evened out slightly. The buck started to speed up, his legs moving him into a slow run. I kept up but remained far enough behind that if I had to slam on the brakes, I wouldn't hit him. Obediently, we followed behind for about another mile.

When we approached civilization, or at least a house, the buck gave us one more final look before turning and trotting back into the trees.

"Should we discuss this or just let it be?" I said. I slowed to a crawl as we approached the house.

"The deer? No, I don't think there's anything to say."

"Me, either."

The house was a big log cabin, or at least built to look that way. It was set at a strange angle to the road. I realized that the angle was for the solar panels on the roof. There were ten panels, and the sun probably rode over them pretty evenly as it moved across the sky, no matter what the season. The woods also appeared to have been cleared back enough to give the panels full exposure. It seemed well thought out.

A second glance, though, told me that everything wasn't as great as all that. There were two window screens hanging loosely from top-floor windows. The front door looked warped but I chalked that up to an illusion made by the house's funny angle.

The yard wasn't taken care of, which wasn't something I'd typically notice. But along with the window screens, the shaggy yard contributed to the general sense of neglected upkeep.

"People do live here, right?" I said.

"That's what Mom said."

"I don't see any cars. Or bikes for that matter," I said.

Before Allison could respond, the front door opened wide. I hadn't noticed that there was a screen door, but when it swung outward, it slammed into the house with a loud metallic rattle that was forceful and not welcoming.

An older gentleman exited the house, his head down and his steps solid and sure. His short gray hair was thin but shaggy, and his white tank top didn't look so white anymore. He wore what looked like a brand-new pair of jeans. They were dark and stiff, and had to be stifling in the summer heat. The jeans were so new it was more like they were wearing him than he was wearing them.

He stopped abruptly when he looked up and saw us. "Help you?" he yelled. "You lost?"

I leaned out my open window and said, "We're looking for Nick."

"That's me. Pull on up to the lawn. Don't much care for formalities around here."

No matter the invitation, I could not, in good conscience, pull my truck onto his lawn, even if it was made up of scraggly weeds and dirt. I did pull up to the edge of the road and parked facing the wrong direction so he wouldn't think I was a complete conformist.

Nick put his hands on his hips and watched us with a one-eyed squint as we started our approach to the house.

He gave in and met us partway, probably after he decided that neither of us could possibly be dangerous.

I had a moment's thought that Allison and I should work on not appearing so harmless, particularly when we ventured out to the edge of the woods to visit a stranger.

"I'm Nick, so I guess I'm who you're looking for," he said with an extended hand.

"Hi, I'm Becca and this is my sister, Allison. We're from Bailey's Farmers' Market."

"Oh, where my Betsy works?"

"Yes." I didn't want to be the one to let him know about the departure note.

"All right. Well, do you know she doesn't live here?"

"We do. We're here . . ." I glanced at Allison, who was looking back at me with confident support. "Well, we're sorry about your brother."

"Oh. Sure. Okay, yes, it's been some rough news." He squinted one eye again and scratched a spot above his right ear. "I'm impressed by your care for your fellow market workers. To come all the way out here to give me condolences. Gosh, that's . . . ladies, I gotta be honest, that's weird. I think you're here for another reason and I'm not one to ever beat around the bush. Just tell me what's on your mind."

"Yes, I'm sorry. We are here for another reason. We're not here officially, though. Do you have somewhere we could sit and chat a minute?" Allison said.

He looked back toward his house and then back at us. "Tell you want, go on around the house to my back patio and I'll bring out some iced teas, unless you'd prefer something stronger?"

"Tea would be great. Thank you," Allison said.

It was a relief on all our parts that we didn't walk through the house—no matter how curious I was about the inside. We didn't know him and he didn't know us and going inside didn't seem like the best idea. Allison and I trekked through some tall itchy weeds and over uneven ground on the side of the house, but once we got around to the back, we were transported to a completely different place.

The back deck extended out from the entire width of the house. It was outfitted with a modern outdoor kitchen and comfortable cushioned patio furniture. The furniture was placed around an unlit fire pit and it faced a picturesque woodsy scene. I looked for the buck but I didn't see him or any other wildlife.

The kitchen had stainless steel appliances that included a six-burner gas grill that made me want to call Sam over to fix some steaks.

"This is unbelievable," I said.

"I know," Allison said.

"Have a seat," Nick said as he came out from the back sliding doors holding three plastic yellow cups with the fingers of one hand and a glass picture full of tea with the other.

Allison and I sat side-by-side on one of the couches as Nick held out the cups. They were all filled with ice, and a second later Nick had topped them off with tea.

Once his own cup was full, he sat down on a facing chair and said, "What's up, ladies?"

"First of all, this backyard . . . your patio and outdoor kitchen are spectacular," I said.

Nick laughed. "Thanks. I built everything myself. Got the

appliances after a restaurant in Smithfield went out of business. I like to see just how much I can power with my panels. My house is one big experiment."

"How's it working for you?" Allison asked.

"So far, so good." He shrugged. "I like living out here. So did my wife."

"Yes, we're sorry about that too. Betsy was upset. Our condolences," Allison said.

Nick blinked hard a couple times, more upset about the months-ago death of his wife than the recent death of his brother, but that was probably natural.

He continued, "Thank you. Betsy likes her small farm but she can't understand my obsession with everything solar, or why I'd want to live so far from town. It was just me and Kristie out here. She liked it."

He didn't allude to any sort of familial issues with his daughter, but why would he mention such things to us?

"We saw a beautiful deer as we came down the road. A buck," I said.

"You did? I'll be. People tell me that all the time, but I've never seen him. I'm not a hunter, and though I like my view of the woods, I don't go traipsing around in them very much. I like to look from the comfort of my chairs." He patted the wooden armrest of the one he was sitting in.

"He came out to the road and actually led us here. It was magical," I said.

"I'll be."

I couldn't tell if he was truly perplexed by the buck's role of tour guide or if he was just pretending to be. I couldn't figure out why he would pretend, but there was something off about him. He was friendly, but he was also wary, maybe nervous, most likely suspicious of us. Maybe just sad he'd lost his wife and brother in the same year.

"Nick," Allison began, "we have some sensitive questions to ask you. Do you mind?"

I blinked at her. Blunt wasn't her style, but maybe she was getting the same vibes I was getting and didn't want to stick around, or be in the way, any longer than we had to.

"All right. I might answer." He took a sip of his tea and looked hard at Allison over the rim of the cup.

"You and your brother didn't get along?" Allison said.

"We got along fine."

"I mean, there was a problem with the solar panels and approving them."

"That was a long time ago. As you can see, I won."

"Right. Well, can I ask if the bad feelings lingered?"

Nick laughed. "I didn't kill my brother. Okay, we hadn't really spoken on friendly brotherly terms in some time, but I didn't kill him. I suppose that's what all this is leading to."

I sat forward a little. Neither Allison nor I were qualified to be asking these questions in any formal capacity, but I got the feeling she'd been more forceful than necessary.

"Nick," I said. "We love Betsy. She's one of the most beloved vendors at Bailey's."

"I'm not surprised. She's a good person," he said.

Maybe my method was worse than Allison's but I continued.

"The other day, the day before Robert was killed, he was at the market and he and Betsy got in some sort of argument. We don't know exactly what it was about but Robert had said something about her business license not being up to date. The next day, Betsy left Bailey's. She just put a note on her table that she was leaving and she packed up. Do you know anything about whatever problem that was?"

"I don't. And it seems to me you're trying to dig around in stuff that's none of your business, and frankly, I'm offended," Nick said.

He took a sip of tea but didn't make a move to get up to throw us off his property, so I continued.

"Not at all," I said. "Betsy couldn't hurt anyone. She simply isn't capable. And like you said, your problems with Robert occurred a long time ago. No, what we're trying to do is understand Robert. He had a reputation as a nice guy." I didn't really know how far that reputation spread, but that's what I'd gleaned from the few people I'd talked to about him. "And we're not so sure that's true. We're just trying to understand him."

"Why? What's it to you?"

I looked at Allison, who gave me a quick nod of approval

"Our cousin is suspected of killing him. We're having some trouble convincing the police that she's innocent, but we think she is. We're grasping for straws, but maybe if we can understand your brother better, maybe we can find a different suspect—or just find something that proves our cousin is innocent. Though we don't mean to point any fingers at you or your family."

Nick took another drink and swirled the ice around in his cup as he looked at us. Finally, he shrugged.

"Well, ladies, now at least I understand what you're doing. Makes more sense why you're here. However, I mentioned at the beginning of this conversation that I like the up front method better. Wish you would have just told me that at the beginning."

I opened my mouth to apologize, but he stopped me with a raised hand.

He continued. "My brother wasn't a terrible guy, but he was pretty stubborn. The thing about him that might help you the most to understand him is that he followed rules better than any person I've ever known. And he didn't like people who didn't. Okay, here's the type of guy he was: he drove the exact speed limit. Exact. Have you ever ridden in a car with someone who goes the exact speed limit? It's annoying. He took his job just as seriously. Letter of the law. He'd spend hours thinking about how to make some sort of stupid regulation clearer or some such thing. It was his obsession. Like I said, we hadn't talked much in years but I know he still thought I was breaking some sort of law with my panels. He couldn't let it go and he couldn't believe the town council would rule in my favor."

Nick sat forward and put his elbows on his knees and looked off toward the woods as he took a moment to think. Soon, he turned his attention back to us.

"If he and Betsy were having a problem, it was something he was taking out on her because of his issues with me. I know my Betsy wasn't breaking laws or rules, but she might have been an easy target for him. If that's the case, I'm sorry for her. I'll ask her."

"Have you seen her the last few days?"

"She came out to talk to me about Robert. I'd been trying to get ahold of her. I have three other brothers. Family news gets around. We'd tried to call Betsy, but she hadn't returned the calls. She came out and was pretty upset."

"Pardon me for saying so, Nick," Allison said, "but you don't seem all that upset."

"I was. A little, I suppose. It's a terrible, tragic way to die, and he didn't deserve to be killed. But I gotta tell you, if I'd known he was harassing my Betsy, he and I would have had some heated words. Doubt I could have killed him. But maybe."

"What about your brothers?" I said. "I don't mean could they have killed him. I mean, did they get along with him?"

"Well, we're not the closest of siblings. Other than my issue with Robert, though, no one had any real problems. We used to be all about the family barbeques and get-togethers, but we haven't done that for some years. I guess you could say that when Robert and I had the falling-out, we all just kind of quit trying so much. It happens."

I heard a tiny bit of regret in his voice.

"It does," I said as supportively as possible.

"You know what you should do—you should go talk to the other people in Robert's office. I bet they know who he was harassing and for what reasons, who was breaking the rules. As good of a guy as he was, if someone was breaking a rule according to his interpretation he would have done something to get under their skin. It was his way. Yeah, the people he worked with would be the ones to talk to."

"Good idea," I said.

It was a good idea. I'd spoken to them briefly, but that conversation had been more about Jeff than Robert.

"Yeah, I can't really help you much," Nick said.

"I think you've helped us in a very big way," Allison said with a smile.

I had to give her credit. She'd probably started off our

conversation with Nick in such a blunt way so I could swoop in and appear to be the "good cop." I wanted to give her a fist bump, but that would have to wait.

I took another deep breath. This part was more difficult than the part where it sounded like we were asking Nick if he'd murdered his brother, but we were there at his house and still had his attention. I didn't want to miss the opportunity even if my next questions forced our reluctant host to finally throw us out.

"Nick, I'm so sorry about my next question," I said.

He blinked and then raised his eyebrows.

I cleared my throat. "The other day I was covering for Betsy in her stall. I had to put some money into her cash box. It was a twenty. I put twenties under the top tray, so I lifted up hers to put the twenty underneath. I wasn't snooping, I promise. But when I did, I saw two bills that were stamped with past due notices."

"Becca," Allison said as if she wanted me to stop right there.

"I'm sorry," I said to Nick, "but do you know if Betsy is having financial problems?"

The pause was like watching an avalanche start. You knew something bad was about to happen.

"Becca, you already know that those notices were none of your business, I don't think I need to tell you that. In fact, I don't need to tell you anything at all, but I'm going to—only because I don't want you thinking what you're thinking. Those weren't Betsy's bills. I suppose if you'd truly been snooping, you would have picked them up and looked at them and seen my name on them. I'm not going to go into any more detail than that, because I think that's all you need to know about the matter."

I nodded.

"Thank you for your time, Nick," Allison said.

He walked with us through the weeds and around to the front part of the house. All three of us were silent.

We muttered good-byes to each other, and he waved and disappeared back into his house before I put the truck into Drive.

"I'm sorry. I took it too far," I said to Allison.

"Not at all. I just thought I should act like you did. I have no idea if knowing that those bills weren't Betsy's might help Peyton, but now you definitely do know. It's like each new bit of factual information fills in a part of a puzzle, even if I don't know what the puzzle's supposed to look like."

"Wanna go downtown?" I said to my partner in investigating crime.

"Absolutely," Allison said.

I smiled and we fist bumped.

Eighteen

Kyle and Meg didn't seem surprised to see me, but they were busy when Allison and I arrived, so they both waved politely as we took a seat on the small lobby's bench.

They were each talking to someone at the front counter and there were three more people in line waiting to be helped. The two at the counter were women and the three in line were men. I recognized a couple of the men from town, but Allison knew one of them well enough to get up and say hello. They spoke until it was his turn to be helped.

"He's applying for a liquor license," she said as she sat next to me again. "He owns a small café."

I nodded. "No one ever thinks much about all the permits and licenses a town needs to run properly," I said.

"I overheard one of the women at the front. She's here for her beautician's license."

"And there's another one," I said.

"I don't think it will help us solve Robert's murder, but it's interesting to ponder how he was involved in lots of people's livelihoods, maybe only for a short time, but still, he knew lots of people."

"Good point, although that doesn't help to narrow down our suspect list."

"No. It expands it, but that might not be a bad thing, either," Allison said.

We sat for only a few minutes longer before the line and the office cleared of other customers. I hoped we'd have Kyle and Meg to ourselves for a few minutes.

"Becca, right?" Kyle said as we approached the counter.

"Yes, and this is my sister, Allison."

"You run the farmers' market, don't you?" Kyle said.

"I'm the manager."

"It's a great place."

"Thanks."

"What can we do for you today?" Kyle said as Meg stepped next to him.

"We have some more questions about Robert," I said.

"All right." Meg spoke first, but her tone was hesitant.

"I know you could get busy any second," I said, "so I'll get to the point. I know you cared for Robert. You liked him. That's great. Liking co-workers and bosses is one of the keys to a happy life. So anyway, my question might seem harsh, but I really need to understand him better." They both looked at me intently. I continued. "Was Robert a vindictive sort at all? I mean, did he ever take out his anger on people when he thought they were doing something wrong? We hear he was a real stickler for the rules, but between us, I have to wonder: if he was such a stickler, why did he let our baked potato vendor drag his feet for so long?"

Meg and Kyle looked at each other. Meg gave Kyle a look that said, "I'm out" before she stepped away from the counter and went back to her desk. Fortunately, Robert turned back to me and Allison.

"Robert was a really great guy," he said. "Really great."

"We got that," I said.

"But he *was* a stickler for the rules—and the rules he mostly stuck to were the ones he thought he interpreted better than everyone else. I wouldn't say he was vindictive so much as he . . . okay, well, maybe sometimes his behavior was a little vindictive, but he thought it was for the greater good. There was no convincing him otherwise. As for your vendor, well, he was stumped there. He wanted to be right— he always wanted to be right, I guess. But he was careful with that vendor." Kyle sighed. "I think that more than being a stickler, more than being right, he never wanted to be proven wrong about something that he thought he should know. He moved slowly with your vendor because he couldn't get the confirmation he wanted to have to take more drastic action."

"Can I ask how he behaved vindictively sometimes? The little ways?" I said.

Kyle looked around to see if anyone else had magically entered the office. Of course, no one had.

"Silly stuff. Petty stuff. Maybe he'd have us misspell a name or something. Like, just a few minutes ago, I helped someone put together their application for a liquor license. If Robert had been here, he would have had to later give me his opinion regarding whether or not that person should have a liquor license. He knew so much about everybody that if he'd found out that that guy had gotten in trouble for something perhaps liquor related, or something similar, I don't know, he would have found a way to delay the license or maybe even find a way to make sure it didn't get put through at all."

"He would judge everyone personally?" Allison said.

"Well, yeah, but not everyone. It's wasn't as bad as that. Most people were just fine, got sent through the process without a hitch. There were a few that didn't, though. Just a few." Kyle's eyes lit with a moment of clarity. He realized that he shouldn't be telling us these things, but like someone with a secret, it felt good to share, to get it out there.

"Any chance you'd want to tell us who those few were?" I said before he stopped talking altogether.

"No. I couldn't do that. That would be violating the trust of the population of Monson. I'm not going to do that."

I nodded. "Let me ask you something very specific. I understand if you don't want to answer, but I don't really think your answer would be a violation of trust. In fact, your answer could potentially right some wrongs."

"I'm listening."

"Were two of the people he was harassing our vendors, Betsy and Jeff?"

"Maybe."

"What was he doing?"

Kyle bit his lip and rubbed his chin. "I can't say exactly, but it wasn't so much what he was doing as what he was threatening to do."

"Now that he's gone, those threats won't be carried out, right?" I said.

"Not unless our new boss wants to do something. We can't control who gets hired or whatever grudges they bring to the job." There went his eyes again. He was going to kick himself later for sharing so much, and I had no idea how to tell him that he didn't need to worry, that we wouldn't tell on him. Because frankly, we might.

"I see," I said.

"Do you have Betsy's renewal?" Allison asked.

"I think we do," Meg said from behind her desk.

Her tone told me that yes, they had Betsy's renewal, and yes, she knew exactly where it was hiding, and yes regarding the fact that Mr. Ship had told them to delay it. Meg was much better at telling us things with only a few words and her tone of voice than Kyle was.

"Do me a favor. Go ahead and process it now while there's no one manipulating anything. I'm sure it will go through just fine," I said.

"I'm sure it will, too," Meg said as she moved her fingers over her keyboard.

"Good," Allison said. "And I'll get Jeff in here to get his license, too. I'm sure you'll treat him with fairness."

"Of course. Now that Robert's not . . . yes, we will," Kyle said.

"Any chance you'd give us more names?" I said to Kyle.

"No. No chance."

I looked at Meg.

"I don't have any idea what you all are talking about," she said. "I've been busy over here working on stuff for some farmers' market vendor named Betsy."

Allison and I looked at each other.

"You need to tell the police about Mr. Ship," Allison said.

"Nope," Kyle said. "And now I have no idea what you're talking about."

He stepped away from the counter and went to his desk.

I didn't quite understand why they didn't want to talk to the police, but it probably had something to do with incriminating themselves for their own bad behavior, not because of any respect for their dead boss. Did I see a need to get the information to Sam? Did what they told us make me think someone in Monson's population, or Betsy, Jeff, or even Peyton killed Mr. Ship? No. I knew we were grasping at vapors, but if I thought blowing a few vapors Sam's way would distract him long enough to keep wondering who the killer was, I might just do it.

Kyle and Meg were done with us and they both looked relieved when another customer came into the office. I thanked them both as Allison and I left. Once back in the truck, Allison spoke up.

"That does not feel right."

"Not at all," I said.

I looked at my sister. She was another rule follower, so much so that even my minor digressions seemed so much bigger than they ever were. Allison didn't stick to the speed limit, but she stuck awfully close to it. I only did because my truck was speed impaired. If I'd driven anything newer, I was sure I'd have a speeding ticket or two.

But Allison was not vindictive. She didn't need to be. She was just honest enough that you knew where you stood immediately and what would happen if you didn't follow the rules. There were no hidden agendas, no misspelled names.

The biggest difference between Mr. Ship and Allison was that she was also flexible and didn't leave all circumstances up to her own interpretation. She listened to and sometimes took advice. And lastly, she was an extremely fair person, the most impartial person I knew. I knew it bothered her that Mr. Ship had behaved in a way that had hurt people she cared about, her market vendors. Though she didn't have it in her to kill anyone, if she'd learned what Mr. Ship was up to before he died she would have at least given him a good talking-to, and as the beneficiary of some of those talking-tos over the years, I knew he would not have enjoyed it a bit.

She was the good example of a rule follower. Robert was too extreme. In fact, he might have done some downright mean things to people, which might be motive for murder.

"Let's go to Jeff's," Allison said.

"I don't know where he lives. Can you get me there?"

"Sure."

There were no fist bumps this time before I followed her directions to the baked potato vendor's house.

I didn't say it out loud, but I knew Allison was thinking about the same thing I was. If Mr. Ship's killer was someone other than Peyton, chances were pretty good that we knew them, at least in passing. I was ready to point the light of suspicion at someone else. I wasn't sure if Allison was there yet.

Nineteen

I didn't really know Jeff. Allison didn't either but she knew where he lived because she knew where all the vendors lived; it was something she did, memorize vendor addresses. She once mentioned that knowing where everyone lived was somehow comforting, that by giving each vendor their "place" in her mind, she was able to give them a dimension that helped her understand them better.

I was surprised when she guided me to Ian and George's old neighborhood, the Ivy League area. Ian and George had lived on Harvard, but Jeff lived on Princeton.

Like Ian had, Jeff also lived in an apartment behind a house, but Jeff's place wasn't above a garage. It was in what looked like a reconstituted, extra-large backyard shed. It was nice, almost feminine, with dainty white shutters and a light green exterior.

"Adorable," I said after we'd walked directly down the driveway to the back. Allison hadn't wanted to knock on the main house's front door. She decided that she wanted our visit to be a surprise to Jeff even if it meant we offended or bothered the residents of the main house.

"He mentioned that he got this place for a steal."

Allison continued to march forward. I had to quicken my pace to keep up. She reached the front door and knocked—no, pounded—on it.

"Open up, Jeff. It's Allison. I need to talk to you," she said.

There was no sound from inside.

"I know you're in there. Open up now."

"Do you really think he's in there?" I whispered.

"I have no idea," she whispered back. "But if he is, I want him to know I mean business."

She knocked again. "Now, Jeff."

We waited another long, silent moment, but then the door opened. A little.

"I'm not feeling well, Allison, what's up?" Jeff said from the narrow slit he'd allowed.

"You're fine. We need to talk to you." She pushed her way into the small house, or cottage or whatever it was.

Once I got over being rattled about Allison's surprise forcefulness, I followed behind but I did give Jeff an apologetic smile as I walked past him. Maybe it was my turn to be the good guy again, and maybe Allison was beginning to enjoy this way too much.

The inside didn't change my mind about the original

structure being an oversized shed, but just like the outside, the inside was adorable and feminine. Jeff was either man enough to welcome his feminine side or the rent was the steal he'd told Allison it was.

The one big room had a couch, chair, coffee table, and small television on one side and a short single-counter kitchenette on the other side. I assumed that the closed door by the range led to a bathroom, and the ladder attached to the back wall led up to a loft bedroom. I liked it, but couldn't imagine living in it. It was small, there was no garden, and Hobbit and I would undoubtedly get in each other's way.

And despite its adorableness, it was messy. Man-messy, I called it. I'd gone through a couple of ex-husbands with the affliction. Neither Ian nor Sam was man-messy. I'd been appreciative of the fact that they both picked their towels and underwear up from the floor without ever needing to be asked.

"Have a seat," Jeff said less than enthusiastically.

Allison moved some papers off the couch, sat down, and then patted the spot next to her as she looked at me. I sat where directed.

"You have a seat, too, Jeff," Allison said.

Begrudgingly, he sat in the chair and didn't make any effort not to look put out.

"What's the deal with the business license?" Allison asked.

"I explained it already," he said.

"Right. So what's the real story?"

"That is the real story."

"No it isn't. It's time to grow up, Jeff. Tell me what's going on."

Anger flashed in his eyes, but I could see him rein it in. Anyone would be upset about being told to grow up, but at least he was smart enough to realize that my sister was correct; growing up was exactly what he needed to do.

He sighed and looked at Allison.

"It all just got out of hand," he finally said.

"What did?" Allison asked.

"My protestations, I guess," he said.

"Explain, please," she said.

"All right. First of all, I didn't kill that man, I want you to know that."

"I believe you," Allison said.

I wasn't sure she did, but I kept quiet by pinching my mouth shut and sitting on my hands.

"Good. Anyway, I found the clause in the law that I thought allowed me to get out of having to get a business license. I pointed it out to that guy at the office, and I learned quickly that I never should have. I should have just applied for the license and let whatever was going to happen, happen." He paused, found some courage, and continued. "I have a felony on my record, Allison. I didn't tell him that part, but when I pointed out the unclear clause, he took it personally and became hell-bent on figuring out why in the world I didn't want to apply for a stinkin' thirty-five-dollar license. He figured it out easily enough. I was arrested for assault a few years back. Yeah, I beat someone up, but that someone was harming a family member of mine, a family member who didn't want to come forward and let the world know what was going on. Anyway, whatever. I was arrested, I did my time, and was on probation for a year or so. I didn't want anyone—well, I didn't want you, Allison—to find out about my past. I really like my gig at the market. I love Monson, and Bailey's. When Ship threatened to expose me, it turned into a . . . well, a battle. I told him that he couldn't expose me without looking like the complete nosy jerk he was. He said he would get me to apply for the license and then he'd have every reason to know about my past so he'd deny the application. I wouldn't bite on his threat, and he just kept trying to corner me. It got so out of hand. A stupid power struggle. I just should have applied and let it be."

"Yes, that's exactly what you should have done," Allison said. "Or you could have just come and talked to me. We would have figured it out."

"Jeff," I added, "I don't think a felony conviction means an automatic denial of the business license. In fact, I don't think anyone is denied. Unless Mr. Ship wanted them to be denied, I suppose. You might have just gotten the license and no one would have known any better."

"I realize that now," he said. "But it just turned into something it should never have turned into. I'm to blame, too, but holy moly, Robert Ship was sure angry with me. My entire reputation was being threatened, but I did not kill him. I'm sorry, Allison."

"You need to go down to the business office today and apply for that license. Today, Jeff. I'm sorry for what you've been through, but you won't be welcome back at Bailey's until you have the license. I check references on all new vendors. I knew all about your arrest and conviction. I know more of the story than you probably want me to know. I haven't told anyone, and from what I learned, you had every right to be angry at the man you hurt. Every right, but you still should have come to talk to me about it."

I thought Allison was more disappointed in the fact that a couple of her vendors hadn't trusted her enough to discuss their problems with her than the problems themselves.

"I understand," Jeff said. He didn't show any surprise over Allison's knowledge of his past. He probably realized how dumb he'd been, knowing that Allison was always thorough and checked references along with past criminal records. "I'm really sorry."

Allison nodded but didn't say that she accepted his apology or that everything was going to be okay. She would wait and see how the application process went first. But if I knew her as well as I thought I did, she and Jeff would end up being be good friends at some point in the near future. They'd reach a mutual understanding that would rebuild their trust in each other, and that trust would never again be broken. Again, it was just one of those things she was good at: forgiveness.

I felt like I should add something so I said, "Love your potatoes, though."

For a beat we were all silent, but then we laughed together.

Allison had had her say. It was something she knew she should have done long ago. She'd either forgotten or ignored Jeff's licensing issues for other, bigger issues that needed her attention.

"It was one of those things I thought would just get taken care of," she said when we were back in the truck. "I didn't see why I needed to intervene. Jeff and Robert Ship should have resolved it quickly. It's ridiculous what ultimately happened. No detail is too small, Becca."

"Do you think he could have killed Ship?" I said.

"Actually, I think he *could* have, he does seem capable of such a terrible thing. But I don't think he did," Allison said. "Nevertheless, I'm going to tell Sam what I know about his past and what we now know about the power struggle between him and Ship. The police can then go talk to Kyle and Meg from that angle. No matter how the police talk to them, they need to be talked to. Mr. Ship should not have been able to get away with whatever he got away with. Kyle and Meg might not need to get in trouble but it's now their responsibility to bring to light all the times Ship got in someone's way."

"You're pretty smart," I said.

"Nah, just been around you enough to learn some of this investigation stuff."

"So far, you haven't been shot at, stabbed, or punched, so you're doing a much better job."

"Oh, there's still time. Where to next?"

"A place I hadn't thought about until we were in there talking to Jeff. I have a new idea."

"Let's go." Allison put on her seat belt.

Twenty

I'd never banked at American Investors Bank and Trust. It wasn't that I didn't like the bank. I didn't have feelings about it one way or another. I just didn't know the bank. My parents had banked elsewhere for as far back as I could remember, so when it became my turn to set up my own accounts, I went to the place I was familiar with.

And I didn't know Lyle Manner. The first time we'd met was in Bailey's parking lot earlier that week. I'd seen him and Peyton having a moment I'd interpreted as somewhat heated, and now I'd heard that Peyton was explaining her lack of a business bank account to him. From a bank man's point of view, that might be a good reason to scold. However, I doubted he would have treated a dumb young man the same way he'd treated my dumb young cousin. Girl power aside, I didn't have an opinion about Mr. Manner.

"Do you know him well?" I asked Allison as I parked the truck.

"Not well. We've worked together for years. This is the market's bank. I've never socialized with him."

"But you didn't work with Robert Ship much?"

"No, not at all. I would never have been the one to apply for the market's license or the vendors' licenses. I saw him enough around town and at the market that I knew he lived in Monson, but I didn't know what his job was. I doubt he and I ever had a real conversation other than the day he came to help with the food trucks."

"Let's go . . . are you Holmes or Watson?" I said.

"You should be Holmes. This is your idea. I'm just along for the ride this time. I'll be your temporary Watson."

"That works."

I always stood out when I went someplace to conduct business when I was dressed for the market: My overalls, short and long, did not give me the air of someone who had any business savvy. I might not have been a Rockefeller, but I knew business, even in my overalls. Nevertheless, I was used to people in places like banks turning and looking at me funny when I came in. Today, though, I had my well-put-together sister with me. She worked at the market, too, but she was always dressed in business casual and there was something about the way she carried herself that made people immediately think she knew exactly what she was doing.

There was more confidence in my steps with her beside me.

"He's over there," I said out of the side of my mouth when I spotted Lyle Manner sitting behind a desk in the back. He was alone in a small glass wall enclosed office and his attention was so focused on something on the desk that he didn't see us enter the bank or approach him.

"Do you want me to say anything?" Allison asked out of the side of her mouth.

"Oh, I got this one, Watson. Just play along."

"I can do that."

We stopped at the open doorway to the office. I knocked on the door frame and said, "Excuse me, Mr. Manner?"

He looked up with a grimace, though I didn't think it was a reaction to seeing us. He was upset, or had been upset. His eyes were circled in black and his mouth was drawn down.

"Yes? Oh, hello, Allison and . . . Becca. Come in." He stood and motioned for us to sit in the two chairs on this side of the desk. He sat again after we did. He tried to paste a patient, good customer service look on his face, but he failed.

"Are we disturbing you? I'm sorry," I said.

"No, I'm sorry. I should have stayed home an extra day or two. I'm afraid I've been grieving my friend and I'm not able to hide it well. Everyone here says I look like a vampire in the making." There was humor to the words but not to his voice, so none of us laughed.

"You and Robert Ship were good friends then?" I said. "I'm sorry for your loss."

"Thank you. Yes, in fact, he and I were very good friends. We'd known each other for years and because of our jobs had many occasions to be at the same places at the same time. Before we knew it, we were also socializing together. After Robert's kids moved away he became Uncle Robert to my two girls. We will all miss him."

I shifted in the chair. I really did hate to bother someone who was so clearly upset, but I also didn't want to miss my chance.

"Did you know much about his brothers?" I said.

Mr. Manner blinked and his eyebrows came together. "Well, not really."

"I guess I mean his brother Nick and the solar panels issue?"

"Oh, yes." Mr. Manner smiled. "We often laughed about that one. Robert had been so adamant that the panels were against the law. When the city council voted in Nick's favor, Robert could only chuckle at himself. He mentioned that the whole ordeal had made Nick so angry that they were no longer speaking."

"I see," I said.

It was easy to be blind to the faults of those we cared about. I understood that, and I wasn't even so sure Lyle Manner had been blind. He might not have ever had a chance to know the whole story of his friend. Or maybe Nick, Jeff, Meg, and Kyle hadn't told us a totally truthful version of the chapters of Robert Ship's life they'd been a part of. The truth was, as usual, probably somewhere in the middle. But it didn't much matter at the moment anyway.

"Mr. Manner, I have to ask you a question. You might not want to answer, but the answer might be very important," I said.

"Gracious, sounds serious."

"It is. It's about our cousin, Peyton Chase. She's one of the food truck vendors visiting the market."

"I know who you mean."

"I saw you and she . . . having a heated moment the day you and Mr. Ship were at Bailey's to set things up for the vendors. Can you tell me what the two of you were arguing about?"

"Of course. Yes, it's why she was here the morning Robert was found dead. She told me that she didn't have a bank account at all, that she kept all her money hidden in her truck. I was chastising her and told her that she should come to the bank immediately and set up her account. She wouldn't do that, so I pleaded with her to meet me here early so we could get her taken care of."

Hmm. No lie to catch anyone in there, it seemed.

"Yes," he continued. "I was very upset at her and I'm afraid I didn't mince words. I told her she was being irresponsible and, frankly, naïve and dumb. I lit into her more than I should have but she said she had a large sum of money hidden in places all through that food truck of hers. She said she didn't trust banks. Later I regretted how fatherly and adamant I'd been toward her, but I'd been legitimately shocked into doing so."

I looked at Allison. I hadn't meant to spring the news on her. My intention had just been to confirm what I'd heard from Sam.

"I had no idea," she said. "I would have done something about that if I'd known."

"Right, and the sum of money she said she had was horrifying," Manner said. "She said she had over sixty thousand dollars hidden in that truck. I was happy her business was doing so well, but I told her she needed to get that money protected."

The other reason I'd wanted to talk to Mr. Manner was to see if we could get out of him the amount of money Peyton had secreted away. I hadn't even had to ask, but any sense of satisfaction over my Jedi questioning skills was replaced by shock regarding the true amount. Either Peyton had sold a bunch of hot dogs in a relatively short amount of time or she'd gotten that money—some or all of it—in another way. I didn't like thinking what I was thinking.

"Did she tell you anything else? Like how many hot dogs she'd sold or anything?" I said, grasping at more vapors.

"No, but I do think I was pretty convincing. She agreed to meet me here."

"But I imagine you two didn't end up setting up the account?" I said.

"No, other things took precedence, of course."

So that money was still out there, perhaps still hidden in the truck. Allison and I would have to find a way to protect it if we could.

"What about Mr. Ship? Why was he here that morning?" Allison said.

"I'm not exactly sure. But I think a market vendor who also had some banking business asked Robert to meet him, that they'd take care of their paperwork here. A baked potato vendor, I think. Robert and I were going to go to breakfast after business had been taken care of that morning, but our breakfast plans weren't expected to happen that early. I'm speculating a little. Robert mentioned the vendor and a potential meeting at the bank, but he never shared with me a specific time. I can't imagine any other reason he'd be here so early. I told the police as much."

And they still didn't suspect Jeff?

Why would Jeff ask to meet Mr. Ship at the bank? I was sure there were other answers, but the two that sprung to mind were that Jeff either wanted someone outside of the business office to witness any conversation he had with Mr. Ship, or Jeff wanted a place where he might be able to kill Mr. Ship without any witnesses. The bank's parking lot in the early morning hours would be hidden from the world. As I'd already pointed out to Sam, bankers' hours were a real thing.

"No security cameras in your parking lot?" I asked.

Mr. Manner blinked a few times and then shook his head. "It's a travesty, isn't it? We're a bank and we don't have security cameras in our parking lot."

We might need to make another visit to Jeff.

"I see," Allison said when I didn't say anything right away.

"You know, Robert mentioned that he didn't like the vendor, that he'd been trouble, but I didn't get the details. I was just happy to help on the banking end, whatever that meant. I didn't know what banking business the vendor wanted to conduct, but I was ready to accommodate him."

"Did you tell the police that Mr. Ship didn't like the vendor, mention any difficulties between the two of them?"

"Of course."

"Good."

"Allison, I'm still waiting on a couple of the other food truck vendors to come in and set up their temporary accounts. Let's see"—he grabbed a folder from the corner of his desk—"Mel from Paco's Tacos and Hank from Noodle Bowls.

I've tried to call them. It's not necessary that they set up the accounts but they haven't returned my calls, and we really can make it convenient for them. You know, get their money back to their hometown banks. I've made all of those calls. If you get the chance, would you remind them of the opportunity we've extended them?"

"Of course," Allison said.

"Thank you. I thought I'd stop by tomorrow, but a heads-up from you wouldn't hurt."

"Be happy to."

I thought we'd given Mr. Manner a moment's reprieve from grieving, but as he walked us to the door and told us good-bye I sensed that he would fall back into sadness again. It was notable that of everyone—Betsy, Nick, Meg, Kyle, and Lyle Manner, Lyle was the saddest over Robert's death. Or perhaps he was the one showing his emotions the most. The family members, Betsy and Nick, seemed the least upset, but perhaps they were just hiding their emotions.

Everyone grieves differently—something I needed to keep in mind.

Once in the truck again, I said, "What did we learn?"

"Bottom line? We didn't do such a great job questioning Jeff, and though we think Robert Ship might have been a jerk in some respects, he certainly had at least one good and loyal friend. We also know our cousin claimed to have hidden a ridiculous amount of money in her truck."

"I think that sums it up well," I said. "The truck's in police custody now, I think."

"I'll call Sam and say something about being concerned

about Peyton's money. I won't let him know what we're up to, and I'll just act like it's something I already knew about."

"Would it be okay if you didn't do that right away?"

Allison glanced at me. "Oh, of course, the money in Arizona. Sorry, I should have thought. Sure, mum's the word. For now."

"Good."

I didn't say it out loud, but of course I knew we were missing something. We weren't the police. We knew that. We wanted to help Peyton. What we'd learned wouldn't help her, and might throw more suspicion her direction if she really did have that amount of money. We needed better direction. Sam wasn't going to tell me anything else at this point.

But someone else might. I dropped Allison off at the market and told her I was headed home to check on Hobbit.

It wasn't a lie, but it wasn't quite the whole truth, either.

Twenty-one

"*I can see why you love it here so much,*" Harry said when we stopped walking. He took off his hat and peered toward the South Carolina woods that bordered my property.

Hobbit, Harry, and I were up along the ridge above my crops, enjoying the warm but serene early evening.

"Have we convinced you to move here yet? You and Sam might make a great team."

He laughed and put his hat back on. "Not quite. All right, my friend Becca, tell me why you called me out here this evening."

"Maybe I just wanted to invite you over for dinner."

"Maybe, but I think there's more to it. Don't get me wrong, though, those egg salad sandwiches were delicious."

"Yeah, I suppose if I had preplanned my invitation to

dinner, I might have cooked up a little more than egg salad sandwiches."

"It's not the food that makes a good dinner, it's the company. The company was perfect, but itchy."

"Itchy?"

"Yes, itchy to get some information from me if I'm not misinterpreting."

"I'm not good at hiding my motives."

"You don't need to be, particularly with me. I've been as up front as I can be with you. You are welcome to do the same. What do you want to know that you think I can answer, even though I might choose not to answer?"

I started walking again. Hobbit and Harry kept up.

"First of all, do you know what's going on with my cousin? Is she okay?"

"I think she's fine. You can visit her anytime you want. Sam got her a really good attorney. I like him."

"But you still think she's guilty of theft, assault, and murder?" I said.

"Actually, I don't think she's guilty of anything yet, but I do think I'm not ready to stop considering that she *might* be guilty. A person of interest. And maybe now I don't think she's a person of interest regarding all those things, but I can't go into detail."

"I don't understand."

"I'm sorry, but Sam would have my hide if I told any of his secrets, and I've got my own secrets to keep. Remember, I've been as up front as I feel I'm able to be. I don't want to jeopardize anyone's case. Honestly, I don't want to jeopardize your cousin's legal standing either."

"You just made me more curious than I already was."

Harry laughed. "I'm sure."

We walked a little farther, a little closer to the setting sun and the orange-lined sky, when he said, "But I can tell you that Sam is a great police officer. You need to have faith that he'll make sure your cousin will be treated fairly."

"I have faith. In him. I really wish I had as much faith in Peyton. Harry, I've tried to find something that might help her, might prove her innocent of any of the charges, but I haven't had much luck. I hope she hasn't done the things she's been accused of doing."

"Me, too."

I looked at Harry. It seemed he was being genuine.

"Harry, do you know how closely Sam has looked at other potential suspects? Other potential killers?"

"He's looked pretty thoroughly as far as I can tell."

"What about the potato vendor from Bailey's? Jeff? Do you know if he's looked at him?"

"I think so. There was a note in Robert Ship's planner that he was going to meet Jeff at the bank early that morning. Jeff claims that there was no early morning meeting scheduled, and he has a solid alibi as to where he was the night before until midmorning, but I don't feel at liberty to tell you the young woman's name who offered the alibi."

"Right. But there was more to what was going on between Jeff and Mr. Ship. It was a strange misplaced power struggle. Does Sam know all the details?"

"I don't know. Do you want me to plant seeds with Sam? Do you think Jeff is guilty of murder? Do you have any solid evidence?"

"Not really. Maybe I just really want Peyton to be innocent." I smiled.

Harry squinted and smiled back at me. "Of course you do. Perhaps I can ask questions without planting seeds, if you'd like."

"I guess it wouldn't hurt," I said. I wished I'd hid the defeat in my voice but it was too late now.

Harry and I followed Hobbit's lead. Harry was interested in hearing about the process of making jams and jellies, from seed to jar. It was an easy topic of conversation for me to fall into. I didn't give him the long version, but I didn't give him the quick and dirty version, either. If I read him correctly, he was truly interested. He was captivated when I explained how I always started my pumpkin plants indoors, and how there were many summer nights when I'd play matchmaker with paint brushes, pollinating the female pumpkin plants with a little dust from the male plants. He thought my plastic molds that turned a pumpkin into the disembodied shape of a head made for much better fare than typical carved jack-o'-lanterns.

He had no idea that there were specific pumpkins used in baking. Sugar pumpkins were smaller than your jack-o'-lantern pumpkins, their insides easier and a touch sweeter for making pumpkin pies.

I gave him a complete tour of my kitchen. He was most intrigued by the sanitizing feature on my dishwasher.

Talking so much about me had been a welcome break from thinking about murder and Peyton's problems.

It was when we were in my kitchen and I pulled out the shoebox my uncle had stored his recipes in that the real world troubles came back to me and I had another question for Harry.

"The handwritten recipe that Mr. Ship had in his hand—was that really from the restaurant? I mean, it wasn't a copy or something?"

"No, not a copy. The real thing."

"How? I mean . . . well, how?"

"It was taken from the back office of the restaurant. It's been missing since Peyton left her job there. Shortly before it went missing, someone reported seeing her leave the office. Alone. And behaving suspiciously. The only other way the recipe card could have feasibly made it from Arizona to South Carolina was if I brought it along. I didn't, Becca. I know your cousin says I might be framing her; I'm not."

I sighed as I put the lid back onto the shoebox. "I didn't ever think you were, Harry. I wish you were. I wish someone was, but I'm beginning to accept that that's not what's happening."

"I'll be taking the recipe card back to Arizona with me when Sam's done with it, but the good news is . . ."

Harry lifted his hat from his head, slicked back his hair (it didn't need to be slicked back), and then put the hat back on. I'd never seen him do such a thing before.

"What, Harry? What's the good news?"

"I probably shouldn't have gone there," he said.

"But you did! You can't just leave it now. You have to tell me what the good news is."

"Dangit, Sam's not going to be happy with me, but that *would* be pretty unfair to leave you hanging."

"Yes, it would."

"The good news is that of the number of fingerprints on the card, so far none of the prints belong to Peyton. None are Betsy's, either, but she wasn't a real consideration, though it was good to rule her out because of the glove you *found*. Well, that's what I know since I last talked to Sam."

"That is good news. How many different prints are there?"

"Not as many as you might think, but I'm not going to give you a precise answer on that one."

"Okay, well, that's good. The fewer the better to determine that Peyton's and Betsy's prints aren't there, right?"

"It's certainly better than if they were there, Becca, but that's about as positive as I can be right now."

I liked the optimism; I glommed on to it actually. It was good to feel a tiny swell of hope.

We left the kitchen and Harry told me and Hobbit goodbye. He took off his cowboy hat before he scrunched into his rental car and drove away.

For a long moment, I stood on my front porch with my hands on my hips as I looked out over my now dark property. The pumpkin leaves made pointy, spooky shadows with the bright moonlight; the faraway woods were a solid backdrop of trees. There was plenty to do; there was always plenty to do. I was okay on inventory, but it wouldn't hurt to make more.

I looked down at Hobbit, who sat next to me and surveyed the same things I surveyed.

"You up for a ride?" I said to her.

Of course she was.

Twenty-two

A summer weekday evening in downtown Monson was probably one of the quieter times and places in the entire universe.

We were a small town, and though we had a little slice of nightlife going for us, weekday nights at the one downtown bar, The Painted Owl, were filled with mostly empty tables and vacant barstools. I didn't even know the bartender's name, but I'd seen him at the market a time or two.

Hobbit and I had to pass the bar tonight to get to my destination, the police station, but it was only by chance that I looked inside through the front window.

I was surprised to see Officer Vivienne Norton sitting on a stool; so surprised, in fact, that I stopped short, leaving Hobbit to travel a few steps forward before turning back to rejoin me.

"Vivienne?" I said from my side of the window.

She wasn't wearing her uniform. I didn't think I'd ever seen her out of her uniform. She wore simple mom jeans and a white T-shirt. Her hair was a little messy, and I'd never seen it other than hairspray still. Sam's hair was also different when he wasn't in his uniform. Was that a police officer thing, something they taught in police officer school? Secure your hair when your gun is on your waist?

I sidestepped back to the bar's door and opened it, moving inside with Hobbit next to me.

The bartender looked up from the typical bartender pose of cleaning a glass with a towel and said, "I'm sorry. No pets."

I looked around. The bartender, Vivienne, Hobbit, and I were the only ones in the place. "I just want to talk to her for a second." I nodded toward Vivienne, who still hadn't turned to notice me. "If Hobbit can just stay up front, I promise we'll be out of here quickly and she won't cause a problem."

The bartender was probably in his late fifties with a long-banged hairstyle that seemed too young for the beefy face and swollen eyes it topped. He shook his head twice but then said, "All right."

Vivienne still hadn't turned around, so I approached slowly and placed my hand gently on her arm when I reached her.

"Vivienne," I said.

She turned and seemed extra surprised to see me, to see anyone, as if she hadn't even noticed that the bartender had just had a conversation with someone else as she sat there.

"Becca, what are you doing here?" she said lucidly with no sign of slurred speech or unfocused eyes.

"I was on my way to visit my cousin at the station. Do you think they'll let me talk to her?" I said.

"Of course," Vivienne said. "She's being treated like royalty."

I inspected her again, but I didn't sense any bitterness or sarcasm in her words.

I hoisted myself up to the stool next to hers. "You think she's being treated too well?"

"Of course she is—if she's a killer especially."

Again, there wasn't much emotion underlying the words so I just asked. "Make you mad?"

"No, not really. I know she'll be punished if she's found guilty." Vivienne took a swig from the bottle of beer in front of her. There was also a glass there, but it was empty and clean.

"You drowning your sorrows for some reason?" I said.

Vivienne set the bottle down, swallowed, and looked at me. "It's a beer. One beer. Not drowning my sorrows. I have no sorrows. Not really. I just wanted a beer."

I looked at the bartender, who tried to hide the look of surprise he directed toward her, but he wasn't quick enough.

"Come here often?" I said with a smile as I nudged her shoulder gently with my shoulder.

A smile pulled at her lips, and at the bartender's, too, which made me smile along with them.

"Becca, can I do something for you?" she said.

I shrugged. "I don't know. I'm surprised to see you so human is all."

"Police officers are people, too."

"Not really. No," I said. "Sometimes they're almost people,

but when they're working, they're Super-People. They have to be. You're currently not a Super-Person like I've seen you be plenty of times. You're just a regular old person who wanted a beer."

She glanced at me and then looked back at the beer bottle she held between her hands. The smile was gone, replaced by total seriousness.

"I wasn't so super earlier today."

"Uh-oh, did you get in trouble for something?" I said.

"No, but that's not how it should be. I should have gotten in trouble. Sam let it alone."

"I don't understand, Vivienne. That sounds like a good thing."

"No, it wasn't and I'm trying to figure out a way to talk to him about it."

"Just talk to him. He's easy to talk to."

"Yes, but . . ."

We were both silent a moment. I noticed that the bartender was listening closely even though he was pretending not to. I caught his eyes with mine and lifted my eyebrows. He got the hint and moved down to the other end of the bar.

"Vivienne, I'm happy to guide you in the ways of talking to Sam if you want, but I have to be honest, I'm mostly just curious about what happened. If you want to talk about it, I'd love to listen. If you don't want my input, just say so."

She looked at me and then back at the bottle again. She started peeling the front label.

"Your cousin. When we got you two out of her truck. I was so scared, Becca. I didn't want you to be hurt."

I put my hand on her arm. "No one got hurt, Vivienne."

"I know, but I . . . I got scared and I let my emotions get the best of me. I was too rough with her."

"Oh. Well, she wasn't hurt by your actions, was she?" I'd all but forgotten about Vivienne throwing Peyton down to the ground.

"No, she's fine, but that's not the point."

"Okay."

"I should not have behaved that way. Sam should have been angry at me for doing what I did. But he wasn't, and I can't decide if he wasn't because you were involved or if he just wants to let it go."

"Oh, that's easy," I said.

Her head turned and she looked at me again. "All right. Tell me."

"You'll hear about it, and he won't be pleased."

"Right. So you're going to talk to him and tell him to get mad at me."

"Nope." I held up three fingers. "Scout's honor, I won't, but I promise you, you'll hear about it when the case is over. He processes everything, *ev-ery-thing*, and if he thought getting mad at you would help solve the murder, he would have gotten good and mad. But he knows a few things. Peyton's not hurt, and she could be guilty of murder, though I sincerely hope not. Also, you're a good cop and you will beat yourself up much more than he ever would. He's giving you the time to do that. And here you are." I smiled.

"But . . ." Vivienne's eyebrows came together. "I . . ." Finally, her face relaxed and she laughed. "You're right, Becca. Here I am. How did I not figure that out?"

"Our"—I cleared my throat, hinting at a deeper

meaning—"relationship gives me insight into the man that it would be difficult to have otherwise."

Vivienne laughed again. "I'll be."

"Right."

"You know, the two of you are a great couple," Vivienne said. "I saw it the first time I saw you together. I believe Sam was questioning you regarding another murder."

"I probably saw it, too, but it took a little longer for me to recognize it."

"Ian's great, too, Becca. You've been lucky in love."

"I was married twice before, Vivienne. I didn't make good matches with either of them. Maybe I'm getting back some good karma after putting up with some of the things they put me through."

"That happens."

She took a swig of her beer, but I could tell her heart wasn't in it as much anymore.

"Need a ride home?" I said.

"It's one beer, Becca, and I've only had a couple drinks from it. If it would make you feel better, I'll stop now."

I shrugged. "Just be safe, Vivienne. You're too good a cop and friend to lose."

Vivienne shook her head slowly. "I really hope she's not guilty."

"Me, too," I said as I scooted off the stool. "I'm going to go see her now. Maybe I can get some answers."

"Do you really think you can?"

"No, but when has that ever stopped me?"

"Good point."

Hobbit had been doing as I promised the bartender she

would do, and was relaxing by the front of the bar. She stood and joined me as we left. I couldn't remember the last time I'd been in the Painted Owl, but it might have been to pick up one of my ex-husbands who'd had too much to drink. I was grateful that part of my life was over. I left Vivienne there with her mostly undrunk beer and a silent but observant bartender. Maybe Sam and I would have to go there some-time together on a date night.

I knew he was right. I knew we needed the . . . well, we needed not to be in the same house while my cousin was under police suspicion. It made sense, but at that moment and even though I knew he wasn't far away, I really missed him. If he wasn't at work (which I hoped he wasn't because I was just about to go to the police station and I didn't want to force us both into an uncomfortable situation), then he was probably at his house, a mere few minutes' drive away.

Wow.

How was this possible? How could I miss him that much already?

"Uh-oh," I said aloud. Hobbit looked up at me. "I think I'm in trouble."

Hobbit smiled and nudged my knee with her nose before she picked up speed and trotted up the stairs in front of the brick building. She knew exactly where we were. If Sam wasn't inside, Hobbit would be disappointed. Come to think of it, and to heck with uncomfortable situations, so would I.

Twenty-three

Sam wasn't there. Hobbit didn't hide her displeasure, but she got over it when Jimmy, the night shift desk officer, rubbed her ears and gave her a bite from his ham sandwich.

"Hey, Jimmy, my cousin's back there. Any chance Hobbit and I can go talk to her?" I nodded toward the door that led to a hallway and back to the jail's holding cells.

"Hang on," Jimmy said as he rummaged around his desk. "Where did I put that? Oh, here it is." He picked up a small piece paper and looked at it. "Sam told me to say to you when you stopped by—yes, you may go see Peyton but you aren't allowed to give her any food or beverages. He wants you to know that he's not starving her. He's feeding her, but it's policy that no outside food or drink comes in unless he approves it." Jimmy put down the paper.

"Of course he knew I would be coming in."

"Of course." Jimmy smiled. "Go on back."

Happy from the treat, Hobbit trotted contentedly beside me as we went through the doors and down the hallway. She didn't know Peyton well, but since I seemed in a good, albeit curious, mood to see my cousin, Hobbit was also game to see what would happen next.

I pushed open the door to the room with the holding cells and peered in. I didn't want to wake Peyton up if she was resting. She wasn't. From the doorway I could only see her bent legs, as if she was lying down. Once knee was crossed over the other and her sock-clad foot bounced to a beat I couldn't hear.

"Peyton?" I said as Hobbit and I entered, but I got no response. "Peyton?"

I approached slowly, but Hobbit didn't see such a need. She hurried to the cell and inspected the girl inside.

Peyton looked over and jumped at the dog face that suddenly appeared. Then she smiled, sat up, and pulled some earbuds out of her ears.

"Hey, girl," she said as she reached her fingers through the cell and scratched the side of Hobbit's face. "Becca, thanks for coming to visit, and for bringing Hobbit." She pulled her hand back, and her smile disappeared. "Listen, I'm sorry about what I did. That was so stupid. I was scared. I'm so glad you weren't hurt."

"I'm fine, Peyton. Yes, it was stupid, but we're okay." I grabbed a folding chair that was leaning up against the wall and set it next to Hobbit.

"I'm so glad," Peyton said.

I looked around the cell. I would have bet that Peyton was the first prisoner in the history of the Monson jail cells who had been allowed to have an iPod.

My mom had been detained briefly a year or so earlier and she'd been pretty well treated then, too. That was before Sam and I had started dating, but I remember thinking he'd been kind to get her some comfortable bedding and good food.

"Peyton, we need to talk," I said. "Heart to heart. Cousin to cousin if you want to look at it that way."

"Okay," she said, but she shifted on the cot and looked around the room.

"It's just us, I promise. Sam once told me there are no listening devices in here and I'm not going to tell anyone anything bad about you. You're family, Peyton."

I wasn't completely lying. Sam hadn't told me there were no listening devices, but I was fairly certain there weren't. And I probably wouldn't tell anyone that Peyton confessed crimes to me, if, in fact, that was what she ended up doing. But I might. It depended on many things, and I wasn't even really sure what those things were.

But I needed to know. I needed to understand what was going on. She'd actually thought that we could make a getaway in her food truck? That was one of the most illogical ideas I'd heard, and I'd come up with plenty of my own illogical ideas over the years.

Peyton looked at me a long moment, her big brown eyes wide and still glimmering with fear.

"I trust you, Becca."

"Good. Now, tell me whatever you've done. Tell me everything. If I can't figure something out, you know Allison can. We'll fix this somehow, Peyton." I sat back on the chair, stuck my legs out, crossed my ankles, and folded my hands on my lap. Surely, it would be this easy.

She blinked and then shook her head slowly. She looked away from me, but I could still see those pretty brown eyes as they filled with tears.

"Peyton?" I said.

Hobbit sat down and whined at the pretty girl in the cell who was about to cry.

Finally, Peyton looked back up at me. "I know it's hard to believe, Becca. It's even become hard for me to believe, especially with that recipe they found on Mr. Ship. But I haven't done one thing wrong. I never stole that recipe. I never took any money. I wouldn't have hurt my manager, and I could never have killed anyone. Never! I made my own recipe based upon what I thought was in the restaurant's version, but I didn't steal anything. I made it on my own. Take that recipe that was on Mr. Ship, make it, and then taste mine. You'll see they're different—okay, similar but different. I am one hundred percent innocent."

"Then someone is sure doing a good job of making you look guilty, of more than one thing. Honestly, Peyton, I don't think you could have ever killed anyone. Ever. And I'm on your side, but did you maybe do something that led to all of this? Something small that has snowballed?"

Peyton shook her head again. "I worked at that restaurant, Becca. I left and then started my food truck. The accusations started right before I left, but I didn't leave because of them. I'd been planning on leaving. I'd wanted a food truck for a long time. It just so happened that I left right after the manager was accosted, but I didn't even know about it until later, until that police officer started asking me a bunch of questions. He showed that video he has on TV, but that's not me. Maybe it looked like I was leaving because I'd done something wrong, but that wasn't it. I just wanted my own food truck. It's that simple."

"How did you come up with the money for the truck?"

"I saved my tips! I'm not kidding. You should see the place where I live in Arizona. It's a dump, but cheap. I scrimped and saved everything I could."

"How come you didn't have a bank account?" I said.

Peyton looked at me with surprise. "I saved my tips— cash. I saved everything in a coffee tin, just like they do in old movies. I paid cash for the truck. I had to pay cash to my suppliers at first because that's how they operate. They don't give new restaurant owners credit of any kind. Okay, so maybe they would have preferred checks, but they didn't make too big a fuss about the cash. Money's still money. They were still accepting my money when I left."

"You set up a business license?"

"Of course. It's an Arizona license. It's valid and current. They took cash, too."

"Okay, so you didn't do anything wrong, but maybe you made someone at the restaurant angry. Is that possible?"

"I can't think of anyone I made angry. I wasn't a perfect cook, but I got better as time went on. Maybe some people were angry about the accusations, but not everyone. I had people on my side, too, even if it doesn't feel like it anymore."

"How in the world could that recipe have gotten into Mr. Ship's possession?"

Peyton took a deep breath and then let it out. "The options for that answer are limited, Becca. It was either me, or someone else from the restaurant. There are just no other choices."

"No one else from the restaurant is here, right?" I said.

"No," she said with a shrug. "And . . . well, and the only other person who is from Arizona, as far as I know, is that police officer."

She seemed to shrink when she said the words. She must have known by now that Harry and I knew each other. She might not have understood just how much I trusted and cared for him based upon our previous time spent together in Arizona. But I did. I cared for him and trusted him completely. I'd just told him as much this evening.

But maybe that was a mistake.

Really, how well did I know him?

Pretty well, actually. I knew him to be a lawman who was a good man to boot.

But still.

He was the only other person who could have potentially brought the recipe to town.

Wasn't he?

Another thought dinged in my mind, but I didn't want to vocalize it and give Peyton a glimmer of false hope.

"I'll talk to Harry some more," I said, though I had no

idea what else there was for Harry and me to discuss regarding the matters at hand.

"Becca, have Sam talk to Harry," she said, her voice almost too even, as if she was trying hard to keep it that way.

"All right," I said. Surely those conversations had been had.

"Anything else you can give me, Peyton? Anything?" I said.

"I wish there was, Becca. This whole thing is awful. I'd like it to just go away."

"Okay." I inspected her through the bars. "Then tell me something."

"Anything."

"If you used the money to pay for the truck, why do you still claim to have a bunch of cash? The cash you were going to use to set up an account with Mr. Manner."

"Same answer, Becca, except you can add my sales. Saved tips, lived cheap, made money selling hot dogs. My truck is popular in Arizona. My food costs are low. I'm my only labor and I don't pay myself much. I realize my methods are unusual but I couldn't see any other way to make my dream come true. No other way."

I nodded. "What were you digging up behind your truck the other day? You know, in that small plot of land. What did you dig up?"

Peyton blinked and then seemed to shrink some more, but she tried to recover. I'd managed to truly surprise her. I was pretty impressed with myself, though when she responded, I wasn't sure how to follow up my crack questioning technique with an equally successful way to get a real answer out of her.

"I have no idea what you're talking about," she said, blandly but with an undercurrent of defiance.

"I saw you," I said. It was the wrong thing to say. It was as if I'd just challenged her to a dual. Peyton didn't shy away from such challenges. An image of her as a little girl with big curls and clenched fists by her side determined not to back down from anything popped into my mind.

"Wasn't me," she said.

Determined though she might have been, she wasn't very good at lying.

"Okay," I said. "Whatever you say. But, Peyton, perhaps there's a chance you're forgetting that it really was you, and maybe the truth would help clear you from the other trouble you're in. Maybe you'll remember doing what I saw you do, and maybe you'll want to tell me why. I can help, Peyton. You're family. I can help."

"I wish I could tell you something that would help." She looked at me with hard eyes. "But I can't."

The moment was up for interpretation, but nothing pinged for me.

"Peyton," I said one more time.

"Thanks for stopping by, Becca. Be sure to give that cop from Arizona my best."

She turned and lay back down on the cot. She plugged the earbuds into place and moved her ankle up to her knee. She started keeping beat with her foot again.

I'd been dismissed. Rudely so, but more important than

the fact that Peyton had been rude was that she'd been *suddenly* rude, and unhelpful. She'd gone from happy to see me to shut down and silent when I mentioned the suspicious behavior I'd witnessed.

I'd struck a nerve.

I decided it was a nerve I needed to bother some more.

Twenty-four

Again, I was early. I'd reached a personal best this week for being at the market early or on time.

Hobbit hadn't been happy at my alarm, but she would forgive me. Getting ready had been weird. I'd missed Sam even more than I'd missed him the evening before, but I tried not to dwell on it.

I had plenty to distract me anyway.

Once at the market, I went directly to the spot where I thought Peyton had dug something up. In fact, I hadn't seen her dig anything up. I'd just assumed that that was what she'd been doing.

My early arrival to the market was meant to give me some private time, but this morning I had an audience.

Apparently, it wasn't just an old-timer vendors' trait to get to work before the sun rose all the way. The food truck vendors also got to work early. They were all there—except Peyton, of course—their counter doors lifted open and their inside lights illuminating them harshly amid the early dawn gray.

Basha was mixing batter, Hank was cleaning large pots, Mel was browning ground beef, and Daryl was prepping wing sauces. It was impossible to walk past the trucks without the vendors noticing me, so I greeted each of them, spending a few moments discussing the finer points of their morning routines. Fortunately, they were too busy to care much about what I was up to after our friendly greetings, and I didn't think any of them noticed me sneak around them and trudge my way over to the disturbed dirt.

I brought a small flashlight that seemed extra bright because I was trying to be covert. Nevertheless, I shined it boldly into what was left of the hole, and I saw a lot of dirt. Just like I'd seen before. In fact, it looked no more or less disturbed than it had during my first inspection. It didn't even seem wind-blown. I dug around a little. And found nothing. I clicked off the light, sat back on my heels, and looked around.

There wasn't much to see on this side of the trucks. No one cared about this little plot of land. It was ignored, which made it a pretty good spot to bury something. But what? And why?

Though I thought no one had watched me come around, it looked like I had piqued someone's interest. It wasn't the one I expected though. Considering our last meeting, I thought Mel was the one most likely to follow me, but it was Basha who stepped surely in my direction. There was some-thing about her approach that made me think she had a specific purpose in mind, something more than just curiosity about what I was up to.

"What are you doing out here?" Basha said as she stopped in front of me. "And what in the world is so interesting? Why is this such a popular spot? I feel like I'm missing something."

"It is?" I said. "Who else has been out here?"

"I saw your cousin out here, and Daryl and Mel were checking it out, too. I think I also saw that big guy from Arizona with the cowboy hat. What in the world is so interesting?"

"Basha, can you, by chance, give me a little more? Can you tell me who you saw out here first and maybe what they were doing?"

Basha's eyebrows came together and she put her fists on her hips. "Well, let's see. I think I saw your cousin first. Or maybe Mel. Then I saw you. Then Mel and Daryl. Lastly, that big man." Basha looked at me. "You know him? The guy with the cowboy hat."

"I do. He's a police officer from Arizona. I met him when I was down there for a visit."

"He's . . . do you know if he's single?" Basha blinked. She was attempting to look comfortable and modern-woman-like with her question, but no matter how much someone wanted to be a grown-up, asking such a question was never easy.

I looked at her in a new light. She was about Harry's age. She was pleasant, and she made cupcakes.

"He is single, but I'm not sure if he's available. We haven't had that conversation," I said. "I'll do a little reconnaissance and get back to you."

"Thanks, Becca. It's probably silly. I'm from Greenville,

but if he sticks around awhile . . ." She laughed. "I sound desperate. I'm not, but it has definitely been some time since I saw someone who made me curious, you know?"

"I do know. And that's too bad that it's been some time. You're sweet, and you make cupcakes."

Basha smiled. "I'm no spring chicken, but I'll take your compliments and thank you for them. What is going on out here, though?"

"I'm not sure," I said. "I wonder the same thing."

She looked at me like she didn't quite believe me. And I'd been totally truthful. Go figure.

"All right then," she said with a shrug.

"Wait," I said as I stood before she could turn all the way around. "You're from close to here. Do you know where the other food truck operators are from? I knew you were from different places, but I never asked for specifics from everyone."

"Well, I guess I'm not sure, but I noticed that Daryl has his home state business license posted right on his inside wall. He's from North Carolina, I'm pretty sure." She paused. "You know what, I actually asked both Mel and Hank where their licenses were—it's not a question I normally ask. I'm not quite that nosy, but after the man from your local business office was killed, I guess that sort of thing was at the front of my mind. I made sure my license was well posted, and will do the same for my temporary South Carolina license the second I get it. I didn't dislike the man who was killed, but he certainly was adamant about the licenses. Made me double check all my expirations on everything."

I nodded. "Do you know where Mel and Hank are from?"

"No, it was obvious that neither of them liked me snooping

into their business, so they didn't say much and I didn't bring it up again."

"Interesting," I said.

"Not really. Not as interesting as whatever is happening out here."

"Right. Walk you back?" I said.

"Sure."

I was much shorter than Basha, but I was suddenly in a hurry. Her long legs had a hard time keeping up with my shorter ones. When we reached the back of her truck, I told her good-bye and peeled off to walk down toward the other end of the line of trucks. I snuck behind Hank's, crouching to look down at the license plate on the back. Mississippi.

I moved to the back again and hurried to the next slot. There was no back license plate on Mel's truck. I was flummoxed, but moved out, around, and through the next slot, in between Mel's truck and Daryl's truck. Daryl's truck had a back North Carolina plate, but Mel's truck had no front plate.

That didn't seem right.

I ventured through to the other side, the side where the chefs could see me.

"Hey, you okay?" Mel said to me from inside his taco truck.

I hadn't tried to hide, but I wished he hadn't been the first one to see me appear from the slot.

"Fine, how's the browning going?"

"Great," he said. He smiled. "It's not one of the harder parts of making tacos, in case you were wondering."

He was cute and charming. But where was he from? The question was on the tip of my tongue, but my gut intervened and told my tongue not to ask just yet.

I smiled at him as I furtively looked around for a business license. I didn't see anything that resembled one.

"Can I help you?" Mel asked, the charming smile now gone, replaced by a question in his eyes.

"No, I'm good," I said. "Just curious about how you all go about doing what you do."

"I see. Well, probably a lot like you do. One step at a time."

I nodded.

"How's your cute cousin?" he asked as he moved the large pan with browning beef off the burner.

"She's fine."

He set the pan to the side of the truck's small stove top and leaned over the counter.

"Should I ask her out?" he said.

"She's in jail at the moment, but maybe when she's released."

He nodded. "Will do."

Well, that wasn't normal. I didn't know much about human behavior, but Mel's question about my incarcerated cousin and his indifferent follow-up response to said incarceration were not right. Not normal.

"Excuse me," I said. "Gotta get my stall set up."

It was a wonder I didn't sprint to Allison's office. As it was, I moved too hastily, as if I was scared and wanted to get away from Mel, which was partially true.

Her office door was locked, but I knew where the emergency key was located. I looked around, didn't see anyone watching me, and reached up to the top of the door frame. I grabbed the dusty key and fumbled as I unlocked the door.

Thankfully, Allison's computer had been left on, and all

I had to do was move the mouse to wake it up. Before I'd even gotten myself adjusted on the chair, I'd typed into a search engine: Paco's Tacos food truck Arizona.

And only another second later, a picture came up and filled the screen. It was the same exact truck that was outside in the Bailey's parking lot.

"I don't understand," I muttered.

I clicked on "Get to know Paco" and was taken to a new page. The man on the page who was identified as Paco wasn't a blond surfer dude. He was a dark-haired Hispanic man with a wide smile and happy eyes.

I read aloud, "Paco Rodriguez came to the United States only a few short years ago. The greatest day of his life was when he became an American citizen. The second greatest was when he opened his taco truck. Click here to follow Paco's Twitter feed—you can find his truck parked through the southern Arizona area seven days a week."

I clicked on the Twitter feed link.

There had been nothing tweeted for over a month.

I went back to the home page but saw nothing that mentioned any employees—no names, no pictures.

I pulled out my phone.

"Hey, Becca," Sam said when he answered. "I missed you."

"Me, too, but listen to me, Sam. Listen closely."

"I'm all ears."

I relayed what I'd found, and then what I thought I might have found. Sam listened and then told me that he and Harry would be at the market in only a few minutes.

I hung up the phone and sat there, trying to put the pieces together. I had no idea what anything meant.

And I had no idea why Allison hadn't arrived yet, but I knew she wouldn't mind me doing what I'd done.

I closed her office door, locked it, and put the key back up on the dusty door frame, and then meandered back out to the parking lot.

And Mel's taco truck was no longer there.

"What?" I said as I looked at the gaping space, which reminded me of a kid's missing tooth.

And then I noticed that the truck hadn't quite left the lot yet.

I took off in a sprint.

Twenty-five

I'd gotten better. I'd become less nosy and less risky over the last year or so. I was more careful now, but the sight of that truck leaving Bailey's made me forget all those good practices and the promises I'd made to Sam and the rest of my family about taking better care of myself.

I ran at it like it was the last truck off a dying planet.

In all fairness, it wasn't moving very quickly. My experience with Peyton's truck had proved that these vehicles weren't built for speed.

I reached the truck just as it was ambling out onto the two-lane highway. It was turning right so the passenger side door was on my side. I pounded on the door, but it was a tall-enough vehicle that Mel couldn't see who was trying to get in.

The truck stopped abruptly and the passenger door swung open.

"Are you out of your mind?" Mel said to me from the driver's side.

"You can't leave yet," I said, my breathing heavy and fast.

"Yes I can. Get out of my way, or I will run you over. I swear to you I will do it."

"Okay, but . . ." I jumped into the truck and sat on the passenger seat. I closed the door. "I'm going with you."

"No, you're not," he said. "Get out."

"No. You go, I go."

Honestly, the fact that I'd put myself into a food truck with a potential killer didn't even occur to me at that point. The overriding thought in my mind was that I wanted to know the truth. I wanted answers that would prove that Peyton was innocent, and this man could potentially give me those answers. I didn't want those answers to get away.

"Suit yourself, but you're an idiot."

Mel put the truck in gear and started off down the road. I was surprised that his truck was much speedier than Peyton's. I grabbed the seat belt and fastened it across my lap.

"Who are you?" I said.

"Name's Mel."

"You're from Arizona?"

He laughed and looked over at me. "Aren't you the little blond Sherlock?"

"That's where you're from, right?"

"Nope. California originally. Moved to Arizona six months ago."

"Okay, so you might as well tell me what happened. I

know you killed Robert Ship," I said as I grabbed on to the seat and the door handle. It was at that moment that I truly realized the stupid position I'd put myself in.

Oh, you might be a killer? Let me come along for a ride in your truck.

Mel was right; I was an idiot.

"You know nothing of the sort," he said.

"Did you know Peyton in Arizona? Why didn't she know you?"

"Because she's a snotty bitch."

"Hey!"

"You asked. We worked together for two days. I thought she was hot. I asked her out. She said no."

"So you framed her for theft, assault, and murder?"

"Actually, I was only shooting for the theft, but she kept putting herself right there. It was all too easy."

"I don't get it."

"I stole the recipe the first day I was at the restaurant. Your cousin left two days later. About a week later, I heard the owners complaining about her opening the hot dog truck and the sauce she served. All I did was tell them I saw her leaving their office the day she quit. That was it. That was all they needed to have to run with their accusations. She'd ignored me. The day we'd met, she ignored me. I had the recipe. I was going to make it, bottle it, and sell it. But they believed me and went after her. It was pretty priceless, really. Then to top it off, when I went to her food truck in Arizona, ordered her food, paid for her food, said hello, she didn't even recognize me. If you haven't noticed, she seems to not recognize me here, either. What a bitch."

I didn't like him calling my cousin what he was calling her, but I had more important things to worry about. As I'd already noted, this truck could go much faster than hers.

"Mel, you need to pull over. You're going to hurt us both, or worse."

"What difference does that make now? You jumped in for the ride. You get to face the consequences."

I planted my feet as firmly as possible and held on tight to the seat. Someone must have seen us leave. I'd already talked to Sam. The police would be here shortly. We just needed not to wreck. That's what I needed to remember.

"You know, you're right," I said. "My cousin is a horrible person. I'm sorry about the way she's treated you."

"Damn straight."

"She was just under some strain maybe. Starting a food truck has to be hard. It has to take a lot of your attention."

"It's not that hard."

I looked at Mel's profile. His jaw was set too firmly, his eyes too squinted, but at least they were looking ahead at the road.

"How did you get the taco truck?" I had to know, even though I sensed something bad must have happened to Paco.

Mel laughed. "That's another thing. How did your cousin not recognize this truck? It was always parked close to where she parked hers." He took his eyes off the road and glanced over at me. I gulped at the anger and perhaps torment I saw in his eyes. "I went to work for Paco when I left the restaurant so I could be closer to Peyton, and she still didn't pay me any attention."

Obsession. Scary, all-encompassing obsession. I'd never

seen it in person before. It was even worse than in the movies.
Mel's entire life had, at least for a short time, been dictated by
my cousin. And there was something in him that wouldn't let
her go. Was it ego? Was it fear? Or was it just simple reaction
to rejection? I didn't know, but he had become so obsessed
with her that he'd lost sight of reality. Big time.

"Why did you kill Robert Ship?"

"Do I look like Paco?" he said.

I shook my head and looked at him. Had he not heard
me correctly?

"Right. Well, that's who's on the Arizona license. That idiot
Ship wanted to talk to him before he let me sign anything for
a temporary license. How could I have ever predicted I would
need a temporary license? I could ignore the banker, but not
that ridiculously persistent license guy. I overheard that Peyton
was meeting the banker at the bank the next morning. Again,
she made it pretty easy for me to set her up. I called Ship, told
him I was a vendor from the market and told him to meet me
at the bank, that I needed to do some paperwork for both him
and the bank guy, but we had to be early." Mel laughed. "He
asked if my name was Jeff. I went with it and told him yes. So
easy. Killed him and then put the recipe card in his hand.
Pretty brilliant if you ask me. Only problem I almost had was
that Peyton was early for her appointment. She almost saw
me. But she didn't." He laughed. "That was such a rush, getting
out of there."

"Where's Paco?" I said softly enough that he might not
have heard me.

"Had to get rid of him. He didn't want to do this tour. When
I heard that Peyton had signed up, I knew I had to go to. It was

easy to request to go the same places she went. It was a long trip—and she still doesn't even know my name."

I was scared, but a flare of anger shot up my throat and momentarily overpowered the fear. I was angry for my cousin, for Robert Ship, for Paco, and *at* myself.

"Maybe you should have just found another girl," I said, loud enough that he couldn't mistake a word.

"You know, I even tried to be romantic. I wrote her a love note and buried it. I tried to make it a fun treasure hunt. I wanted her to follow clues to see who'd sent it to her. She picked up the note, but she didn't even follow the first clue. She doesn't care about anyone but herself."

"Or she wasn't in the mood for romance, Mel. Not everyone needs that, you know."

"We would have been perfect together."

"And yet you framed her for horrible things."

"She would never have been convicted."

"The police didn't know you were from Arizona, Mel. The recipe card was found in Robert Ship's hand. Who were they supposed to think was his killer?"

"Peyton. But I knew they'd figure it out eventually. I planned to be gone by then, but then *you* got all curious. I knew I should have left yesterday."

"Where were you going to go?"

"I was going to hide. I would have thought of something. How'd you figure me out?"

"You didn't have any license plates on your truck. I don't know when you removed them, but that was pretty suspicious. I looked up Paco's Tacos—Facebook and Twitter were your ultimate downfalls."

"If I'd had Paco's passwords, I would have lasted longer."

"Come on, Mel, pull the truck over. This is dumb."

As we'd been talking, he'd slowed the truck down to only a slightly unreasonable speed, but my request managed to remind him that he was supposed to be escaping. He pushed his foot hard on the accelerator.

"What—you'll tell that police officer boyfriend of yours to be easy on me?"

I shook my head. Mel was obsessed, but he wasn't stupid. Telling him I had any control over Sam or any other officer for that matter wouldn't make sense. It was unbelievable even to someone who'd lost their grip on reality.

"I just think it's all bad enough, Mel. Why would you want to make it worse?"

"Once you reach a certain point, nothing is worse."

As if to punctuate his defeatist stance, the noise of sirens suddenly sounded loud and close.

I tried to see out the back of the truck by looking down the inside middle, but the mini restaurant was in the way. I looked out the side rearview window and my heart soared at the sight of a police cruiser with flashing lights right behind us.

"Come on, pull over, Mel," I said.

"Not gonna do it. You should never have climbed aboard." Mel's voice was maniacal, wicked enough to scare me again and make me double-check my seat belt.

He looked out his side mirror and cursed loudly, causing spit to fly out of his mouth. It was an odd thing to watch—his spit. It landed on the windshield just as the world started to turn funny.

Mel yanked the steering wheel—on purpose—sending us down an embankment. The move was done at a higher speed and with much more intent to harm than Peyton's journey off road.

Mel's truck didn't just bump funny down the hill and then stop harmlessly. The food truck rolled, the sound of the vehicle combined with the sounds of crashing kitchen dishes and utensils. I'd dropped so many bowls in my day that my ears picked out those sounds and focused on them as the seat belt yanked my legs each time the truck was upside down. There were two rolls.

I'm sure I screamed, but I don't remember.

The next thing I knew, I was being pulled out of the now-right-side-up truck.

"Becca, Becca!" Sam held my arms and looked at me, checking to see if I was aware enough to answer back.

I snapped to. "I'm okay, Sam. I'm okay."

He pulled me close, hugged me so tight that I lost my breath for a second, but I didn't want him to know, so I battled through.

We were alone in the world. We were on one side of the truck, but no one else was there with us. I heard commotion. I heard yelling, but it was all happening in that other world on the other side of the truck. On our side, in our world, it was just us and South Carolina countryside.

Sam released the vise grip and held me at arm's length.

"Listen to me," he said. I nodded. "I love you more than life. Just so you know, I would go so far as kill to keep you safe even if you did something stupid and illegal. I would hide evidence. I would plant evidence. I would never, ever let you get in trouble. If you don't already know that, I've failed in showing you how much I care. I would die if something happened to you, Becca Robins. Do you understand that?"

"I love you, too," I said, but the words sounded so wimpy after what he'd said.

"Marry me?" he said.

"Can we do that this afternoon?" I said.

Sam laughed and pulled me close again. "We can do it anytime and any way you want."

"Then, yes," I said, breathlessly and with a slur. He was crushing me again and my lungs and mouth couldn't function quite right.

Not a bad outcome for a dumb girl who willingly got into a crazy person's food truck.

Twenty-six

We didn't get married that afternoon. Sam would have done whatever he needed to do to circumvent things like marriage licenses if I'd wanted to. A justice of the peace would have been easy to find. But we just got too busy.

Other than some seat belt bruising, I didn't get hurt from the truck's two full rolls. Mel didn't get hurt, either, but he certainly got arrested. Sam and I missed it all, but Vivien was apparently even more forceful with him than she'd been with Peyton.

Peyton was released. Harry apologized to her. Vivienne apologized to her. I did, too, though I wasn't at all sure I owed her an apology.

Peyton had no recollection of ever meeting or knowing Mel before sharing parking lot space with him at Bailey's.

And he'd been correct; she hadn't picked up on his name yet. She'd thought of him as the blond taco guy. And she'd had no idea that Paco's Tacos was from Arizona. Neither had Harry. I thought maybe he'd kick himself for a long time for not looking more closely at the food truck chefs. His self-appointed task now was to find Paco's body, and see that his family in Mexico was made aware of his tragic end.

I decided that Peyton needed to work on her powers of observation, which was my way of telling her the she might want to consider being less self-involved. She was young, she was beautiful, and maybe it went with the territory. But it was time for her to grow up and realize there was more to the world than the parts revolving around her.

She'd gotten the note about the treasure hunt that Mel had buried. She said she was so used to men hitting on her that she just blew it off. She didn't want to tell me about it when I asked her while she was in jail because she didn't think it was important. And she thought it was a ridiculous waste of time. She also said she got embarrassed from all the male attention she got. I didn't think that was a lie, but there was something more to it than that, something she wasn't admitting to. I didn't take the time to think about it too much, but I thought that it had something to do with her self-involvement. I hoped that meant she was aware of the chink in her personality, but ultimately, it was something she'd have to come to terms with on her own.

She said that the outside panel of her truck had been squeaking at a spot in the top-right corner. She'd climbed up there and tried to stop the noise, which is what Basha had observed. Peyton had never hidden anything in the tube/pipe. Such an idea had never even occurred to her.

She still claims not to have committed the assault and stolen the money. Harry was going to take a closer look at the restaurant manager who told Peyton not to take the money to the bank for a whole week. That angle is making more sense to him, particularly now that so many other things have come to light. He promised he'd call when he uncovered more information.

Allison had been late to the market because she'd had to take her son, Mathis, to a dentist appointment. But the second after she confirmed I was fine, she grabbed Peyton and made her get all the money she'd kept hidden in her truck. They went to a bank and set up an account. Peyton had been forced to spend alone time with Allison. I could only imagine the lectures. Thinking about it made me smile.

Everyone came to the market that evening. My family, Harry, Vivienne, even Ian and George. We invited Lyle Mannor, but he declined. So did Betsy, though she did tell Allison that if she was able to get her business license taken care of, she would come back to Bailey's. We even invited Jeff, but he'd called Allison earlier to decline and to let her know that he'd filled out and turned in his application.

"You are an interesting woman, Becca," Harry said to me. "I don't understand why you did what you did. Why did you get in that truck?"

"Do you ever hear a funny sound in your house and you know that you are hearing something that every person in a horror movie hears before they're brutally killed but you go check it out anyway?"

"Sure."

"It was like that. I couldn't stop myself. I wanted Peyton

to be innocent so badly that I didn't think about what I was doing. I just did it."

"I should have realized that's what you were like when you were in Arizona. I should never have agreed to our deal to both investigate your cousin."

I laughed. "It wouldn't have mattered if you agreed or not, Harry. I was going to do what I was going to do. Sorry about that."

"I'm just glad you're okay."

"Me, too."

He tipped his hat before his eyes wandered over to the cupcake truck.

"Excuse me, Harry," I said. "I should go see if Allison needs any help."

Allison didn't really need my help, but she was happy to hand me a tray to deliver to Daryl's truck as she carried a giant pot.

"So I guess Mel is in trouble in both South Carolina and in Arizona. Where first?" she said.

"Here. Our murder trumps the other stuff. That's what Sam told me."

"Makes sense." She lowered her voice. "We put about sixty thousand dollars into a bank account for Peyton. Do you think it's actually money she earned?"

"I think so. I hope so." I spied Peyton talking to Ian and George.

"She must be really good at scrimping and saving; that's a lot of money."

"It is."

"Maybe Harry will figure it out."

"If anyone will, he will."

We delivered the tray and the pot and then I helped Allison set out some battery-powered lights. The parking lot by the remaining trucks turned into a party zone. The truck chefs served the food—Allison told them the market would reimburse them for everything they served this evening. Sam had to attend to some business so he got there a little late, though he arrived dressed as casual Sam, not official Sam, which pleased me.

By the time he arrived, I thought I'd listened patiently to everyone's lectures about my behavior. My parents, Allison, Harry—no one was happy with what I'd done, but they were all grateful I was okay. All's well that end's well, or so I said a hundred times or so.

Daryl and Hank had no idea what type of person their new friend Mel truly was. They'd spent the evening apologizing to everyone and being baffled that they hadn't seen it.

That day I'd seen Hank just appear from between the trucks, when I thought he was behaving strangely, he was, but his behavior had nothing to do with Peyton or the canvas bag. His truck had been deemed okay by the food safety inspector, but one of his refrigerators had suddenly stopped running. He was worried he was going to be shut down—what I'd seen were his concern and his mind working through how he was going to fix his problem. He did fix it and the food safety inspector never even knew it had broken.

I introduced Harry to Basha, and thought I saw a little spark between the two of them. Maybe, maybe not. All I could do was make the introductions.

The other spark I saw worried me. Not only did Peyton

seem to know Ian's name, but she seemed to pay way too close attention to him and hang on his every word. They were both over twenty-one and it really was none of my business, but I hoped that Peyton decided to go back to Arizona soon, just for Ian's sake.

"Hey," Sam said as he snuck up behind me while I was talking to my parents.

I faced him, went up to my toes, and kissed him way too passionately considering my parents were in the general vicinity.

True to Jason and Polly, they went with it.

"Goodness, Becca, let the man breathe," Dad said.

"I don't know, Jason, he doesn't seem to mind," Mom said.

"Not even a little bit," Sam said. He turned to my parents. "I don't want to be rude, but can you excuse us a second?"

"Of course," Mom said with a smile.

She'd been supportive of all my husbands and boyfriends, but there was something in her smile I'd never seen before when it came to one of my significant others: relief.

It was something I might need to ask her about, but for now I just took Sam's hand as he led us through the parking lot and to my truck. It was parked close to the office building and far enough away from the party that no one there would notice us.

Sam helped me into the bed of the truck and then jumped in behind me.

"What's this?" I said to the two lawn chairs and the bottle of apple juice chilling in an ice bucket.

"Have a seat," Sam said.

I sat as he sat on the other chair and took my hand.

"I meant it, you know. That was a real proposal, but I thought I should solidify the offer. I was going to take you someplace wildly romantic, but then I realized that this was better. Your crazy old truck, the Bailey's parking lot, your family close by." He tapped on the back cab window and Hobbit popped her head up and smiled and panted a greeting. "I even grabbed her."

"Hey, girl." I patted her head. I turned to Sam. "How did you get her to do that?"

"Told her the plan. She agreed." Sam shrugged.

"Sam. This is perfect. You were right."

"So what about it?" He moved down to one knee, shoving the lawn chair back with a clatter. He reached into his shorts' pocket and pulled out a ring. "What do you think, still want to marry me?"

The ring was simple, and beautiful, the diamond embedded more into the band than on top of it. I would be able to wear it at Bailey's, or working in my kitchen. It was perfect, too.

I looked at Hobbit, I looked at my family and friends just far enough away, and then I looked at Sam. It was a perfect South Carolina summer evening.

Life could be so unpredictable.

"As soon as possible," I said.

Recipes

Basha's Pucker-Ups

These are the lemoniest of all lemon cupcakes ever. If you merely like lemon, stay away from these, but if you *love* lemon, these are your cakes.

CUPCAKES

1½ cups all-purpose flour
1 teaspoon baking powder
½ teaspoon salt
1 stick unsalted butter, melted
1¼ cups sugar
3 eggs
1 tablespoon vanilla extract
¼ cup lemon juice
½ cup whole milk

FILLING

*½ cup lemon curd (find it by the jams and jellies in your
    grocery store)*

FROSTING

3 cups confectioners' sugar
1 cup unsalted butter, softened
1 tablespoon lemon juice
2 tablespoons heavy whipping cream

Preheat oven to 350 degrees. Line cupcake tins with liners.

Whisk flour, baking powder, and salt together in a medium bowl.

Mix together melted butter and sugar with a hand mixer for about 30 seconds. Add eggs one at a time, mixing after every egg. Mix in vanilla extract and lemon juice.

Alternate adding flour mixture and milk, mixing after each addition but just until mixed. Don't overmix.

Fill cupcake liners ¾ full. Bake for 13 to 18 minutes until toothpick comes out clean. Cool completely.

Scoop out a small amount from the middle of the cupcakes, about the size of a marble, and fill with lemon curd, about ½ tablespoon.

To make the frosting, place butter in a medium bowl. Add confectioners' sugar a little at a time, mixing each time until sugar is coated. Mixture is ready when it is creamy.

Add lemon juice and whipping cream and mix until all ingredients are combined and creamy.

Frost the cupcakes and serve. (This is a lot of frosting. Some people like to pile it on. This amount will accomplish that.)

Makes 15 to 16 cupcakes.

Asian Ramen Bowl

½ pound boneless, skinless chicken breasts, cut into
    cubes
¼ cup water chestnut halves
½ cup snow peas
⅓ cup bean sprouts
¼ cup celery
3 tablespoons oil
1 package Oriental ramen noodles, with seasoning
    packet
soy sauce to taste

In a frying pan, brown chicken until done all the way through. Add water chestnuts, snow peas, bean sprouts, celery, and oil. Sauté until vegetables are tender.

Cook noodles according to package directions and drain. Add seasoning packet. Spoon chicken and vegetables over noodles and sprinkle with soy sauce.

Makes 2 servings.

Mel's Shrimp Tacos

A seafood twist on tacos.

TACOS

1 tablespoon olive oil
1 clove garlic, minced
¼ teaspoon kosher salt
½ teaspoon ground cumin
20 medium shrimp, peeled and deveined
4 corn tortillas
oil for frying
shredded lettuce
diced tomatoes
sliced avocado
cilantro lime sour cream (recipe below)

CILANTRO LIME SOUR CREAM

¼ cup sour cream
2 tablespoons chopped fresh cilantro
¼ teaspoon cumin
juice and zest from 1 lime
salt to taste

In a bowl, whisk together olive oil, garlic, kosher salt, and cumin. Add in shrimp and toss to coat completely. Cover and refrigerate for 20 minutes.

Cook shrimp in skillet on medium heat until pink and cooked through, about 5 minutes. Turn off heat and cover to keep warm.

Coat the bottom of a small pan with oil, about 2 tablespoons. Heat over medium-high heat. Cook tortillas in pan one at a time until soft, about 30 seconds on each side. As you cook each tortilla, place them on paper towels to absorb any of the leftover oil. Then fold over to make a taco shell.

In a separate bowl, mix together all the ingredients for the lime cilantro sour cream.

Spoon 5 shrimp into each taco shell. Top with lettuce, tomato, avocado, and cilantro lime sour cream.

Makes 4 servings.

When Pigs Fly Wings

This isn't much of a recipe, so I'm going to call it a bonus "idea." It's the simplest thing you'll ever make, and one of the yummiest, particularly if you like bacon and all things bad for you.

Lawry's Seasoned Salt, just a little
bacon, pieces equal to the number of chicken wings
frozen chicken wing sections, you choose the amount

Preheat oven to 375 degrees.

Sprinkle a little of the seasoned salt over one side of each piece of bacon. You don't need a lot, the bacon is naturally salty; this is just to give it a slightly seasoned flavor. Wrap each chicken wing with bacon, seasoned side inside. Place all the pieces on a baking sheet—make sure it has sides. Bake for about an hour or until the internal temperature of the chicken reaches 185 degrees.

Serve alone or with other dipping sauces. My favorite sauce for these wings is either plain honey or honey mustard.

Thing to remember about this recipe: A little goes a long way.

HOT DOGS

The combinations of toppings are endless, but below is a selection that would make any hot dog food truck vendor proud.

You can boil your dogs and put them on a bun, but the favorite method in my family is butterfly slicing the dogs, grilling them, and placing two regular-sized dogs on one slice of soft white bread, and then adding the toppings. You can either eat them by folding over the piece of bread or using a fork.

Don't forget, there's nothing wrong with the basics: ketchup, mustard, relish, chopped onions.

CHILI CHEESE DELUXE

You can't beat the combination of chili and cheese on a dog, but switch it up a little and make it macaroni and cheese and chili. Give it heat with a splash or two of hot sauce or keep it mild.

CHEESY DOG DELUXE

Macaroni and cheese and tomatoes, or ketchup if that's your fancy.

SOPHISTICATED LADY

Sautéed mushrooms and sliced onions. Sauté them together in some olive oil over medium heat. Keep them over heat long enough to let the onions become sweet. So good. Add a little spicy mustard if you like a kick.

NACHO DOG

Cheese, black olives, broken-up tortilla chips, and (here's the best part) French onion dip. The mix of sour cream and onions is perfect. You can add some salsa, too, if you want.

ASIAN DOG

Grilled pineapple and teriyaki sauce. Yeah, grilled pineapple. If you haven't tried grilled pineapple yet, you should try it soon, either on dogs or not.

WINE TASTERS

Gouda cheese and grilled red seedless grapes. Slice the grapes and grill them inside down. Simple but very flavorful.

GREEK DOG

Kalamata black olives, feta cheese, and tomatoes. Sometimes I drizzle a little olive oil and vinegar onto the bread.

CHEESY CRUNCH

Macaroni and cheese and crushed-up potato chips. Tomatoes sometimes, too.

THANKSGIVING DOG

Stuffing (Stove Top is fine) and cranberry sauce, or jelly. Yeah, it's pretty good.

CHICAGO DOG

The typical Chicago dog is topped with yellow mustard, chopped white onions, bright green sweet pickle relish, a dill pickle spear, tomato slices or wedges, pickled sport peppers, and a dash of celery salt. The dog is usually boiled and served on a poppy seed bun, but the ingredients taste good if the dogs are grilled and served on white bread, too.

OTHER TOPPINGS TO REMEMBER:

Dill pickles, but don't forget the bread and butter pickles. Olives—all kinds—and they typically go well with cheese. Speaking of cheese, get adventurous. Try some Havarti, or pimiento spread. Crunch is good, too. French's French Fried Onions are great in place of other onions. Surprisingly, celery is good, too.